GRA

e return / renew
an renew it at
.norfolk.gov
elephone: (
 have you

WILDCATS

He'd lived among whites for thirty years, yet there was a lot of Indian in Jim Santee. His gunspeed and ready fists made him a good and loyal friend — or bodyguard. Governor Burdin blessed the day he hired him. That was until Santee failed a crucial assignment. To make amends, Santee tore the Territory apart and ran the killer down, but shock developments raised serious doubts ... and no gunfighter should reach for his guns if he's unsure of his target.

TYLER HATCH

WILDCATS

Complete and Unabridged

LINFORD
Leicester

First published in Great Britain in 2009 by
Robert Hale Limited
London

First Linford Edition
published 2009
by arrangement with
Robert Hale Limited
London

The moral right of the author has been asserted

British Library CIP Data

Hatch, Tyler.
    Wildcats. - -(Linford western library)
    1. Western stories.
    2. Large type books.
    I. Title II. Series
    823.9′2–dc22

    ISBN 978–1–84782–889–7

Published by
F. A. Thorpe (Publishing)
Anstey, Leicestershire

Set by Words & Graphics Ltd.
Anstey, Leicestershire
Printed and bound in Great Britain by
T. J. International Ltd., Padstow, Cornwall

This book is printed on acid-free paper

PROLOGUE

If the stupid horse hadn't shied at the shellback lizard and thrown her, she wouldn't have stopped at the river to wash the mud off her clothes.

Then, it being so hot, and this place so isolated, with lots of bushes around, she mightn't have been so daring as to remove all of her clothing and lower herself into the cloudy water. It felt pleasantly cool, because the air was thick with humidity and scudding, leaden clouds drooped their way across the sky.

'It's all right, horse — I forgive you!' she called softly, laughing as she lightly scrubbed sand along her golden arms and shoulders. The horse lifted its head briefly, then returned to grazing a small patch of grass.

She began to sing softly and didn't even swipe in annoyance at the few flies that came humming about her. She merely tossed her head several times, flailing them with wet, raven-black tresses, smiling as the insects darted away, startled.

The water came to just below her waist and she lay back now, propped on her elbows, allowing the lazy current to caress her body and limbs. She threw her head back, some of her hair trailing in the river, humming rather than singing, suddenly more content than she had been for hours.

This was just what she needed after the terrible start to her day. Betrayal by a so-called friend is never easy to take.

Her humming faltered a little and the smile that had exposed her white teeth, framed by the red, sensuous mouth, faded slightly. Then, in a stab of annoyance, she shook her body, rippling the water briefly.

'No!' she hissed. 'I will not let that

spoil things! It is almost noon, moving now into a new part of the day — I will make it an afternoon to recall with pleasure: a leisurely bathe in this river while my clothes dry.' She glanced at where she had draped them over some bushes. 'And then I will ride into town, arriving just on sundown. The evening shall bring what it may and tomorrow — *tomorrow* I will adjust things so that this morning's events will disappear from my memory forever.'

Well pleased with her decision, she still felt the surge of anger struggling to rise within her, but by sheer will put it down. 'No! Tomorrow I will be angry again. For now, I will make this hour mine, and mine alone, and — '

Her words stopped abruptly. She stiffened, still supine, with the water washing over her body and limbs.

She heard loud, angry voices on the river's far bank. Lifting slightly, she turned her head towards the sounds. Through the thin screen of brush she saw a group of men kicking and beating

3

another man, who was writhing on the coarse sand, scrambling to escape. They dragged him to his knees, two of them taking his arms and stretching them out, bending them painfully. The battered man turned a bloody face upwards, smashed mouth working in a soundless plea.

A tall man in a frockcoat, fair hair ruffled and awry — he had apparently lost his hat during the scuffle — stepped around behind the kneeling victim, placed the muzzle of a gun to the back of the man's head and, looking at a smaller man who nodded, pulled the trigger.

Then a calloused hand gripped her arm and effortlessly yanked her to her feet, her surprise choking off the cry of horror that caught in her throat.

An unshaven face was bare inches from hers and sour breath reached her, strained through broken teeth as the man chuckled.

'Well, well! Looky here! Christmas, smack-damn in the middle of Ju-ly! Aw, what you got for poor ol' Joe, sweetmeat — ?'

'This!' she hissed, the nails of her free hand raking deeply across his eyes, gouging dirt-grained flesh.

He clawed at his face, staggering and making guttural sounds as she kicked and punched her way free, thrust past him and started to run towards her grazing horse, drops of water flashing silver fell from her glistening, wet flesh.

Across the river, someone shouted.

Two crashing shots were fired. Her horse whinnied and reared, pawing the air before tumbling to the ground, kicking in its death-throes. She sobbed, engulfed by fear.

Now she had no means of escape.

1

Yuma

The man they brought into the small, windowless room in the Yuma Penitentiary South Wing, had been summarily pulled from the chain gang working on a new wall of the exercise yard where it overlooked the Gila River.

And he looked it.

Filthy, with clods of moist dirt and cement powder in his hair, plastering his unshaven face, on his bare, blistered feet with the long horny toenails. The work clothes hung on him like rags — and that's all they were — rags.

Two men were waiting in the room, one seated at the small table, the other standing by the door that was closed now with a clang by the armed guard who leaned against it, face blank and bored.

Seated at the table was a lawman, a sheriff's star dragging at his shirt pocket. He was in his late forties, heavy-featured with big hands and thick fingers tapping impatiently against the pine table top, which was bolted to the floor. His name was Walt Bascombe and now he shuffled some papers and spoke without looking at the filthy prisoner.

'You the one they call Navajo Joe?'

'He's the one, Sheriff,' the armed guard said, leaning against the door, carbine tucked under one arm as he started to build a cigarette. 'Nah-ver Ho-ho-ho Joe.'

The sheriff's bleak gaze swung to him. 'I'm not talkin' to you, Bale — and put that tobacco away. No smokin' in here.'

'Hell, Sher'ff, even the warden lets us — '

'The warden ain't here. Now get rid of it.' The lawman waited until the muttering guard had put the tobacco sack and papers back in his pocket and straightened up, with his carbine. 'Now, again, for the record, you're Navajo Joe?'

'You know me, Sher'ff.' The prisoner sniffed, starting to draw back through his dirt-clogged nostrils.

'You spit on the floor and you can look forward to night latrine duty for a month, you son of a bitch!'

Navajo Joe swallowed and clamped his scaled lips together. The sheriff turned a page, went back to the first one, glanced up.

'Hell, Joe, you ain't never goin' to get outa here before you're trippin' over your damn beard!'

'Think I dunno that? I was set-up.'

'Sure you were — ain't it always the way? But you could find a year or two cut off your sentence, you decide to co-operate with us.'

Navajo Joe tensed, his hands clenching. Slowly he swung his shaggy head towards the silent man leaning against the wall by the door. 'So that's why you're here? I've seen you before somewheres.'

The man said nothing. He was in his thirties, tall and rangy, deeply tanned, like someone who had spent a lot of time in desert country. His face was wolfish, narrow, with a square jaw, and steel-grey eyes. Wide, flat shoulders, lean-waisted: obviously a man who spent many hours in the saddle. His clothes were those of a cattleman, clean enough but unpressed. He wore a single Colt rig, the holster carelessly pushed around his hip towards his back.

That apparent piece of carelessness had cost several men their lives over the years, figuring he would be slow on the draw if he was that casual about packing a gun.

'You — you wanna make a deal with me, Santee?'

The sheriff snorted. 'You sorry son of a bitch! Talkin' like you'll have a say in it! Mister, you only get this one chance. Tell us what we want to know and you *might* lose a couple years off your sentence.'

'Might!'

'We don't give guarantees, Joe.' Santee smiled faintly. 'You help us, I can *ask* the governor's chief justice to show some leniency. But if our timing's off, or it happens to be a bad day, when he's got a hangover . . . '

'Christ! That's *any* goddamn day!' Joe looked horrified, started to get to his feet but when the sheriff dropped a hand to his gun butt, the prisoner eased back in his chair. 'What — what you wanna know, anyway?'

The sheriff glanced at Santee who said flatly, quietly, 'Senator Rankin's son.'

Joe went grey, the paleness showing clearly through the layer of dirt. His head shook violently. 'Hell, I dunno nothin' about that! Lemme outa here! You got the wrong man.'

'Siddown, Joe,' Santee said sharply and the man sagged in his chair, still shaking his head. 'You were there; you know who killed him — we don't. We need proof — from an eye-witness.'

'No, no, you got it all wrong — Judas

priest, I was nowhere near the river when Josh Rankin got it. I swear!'

He was breathing hard and fast, breath wheezing noisily in his dust-clogged lungs. Santee stared levelly at him.

'Joe, you had a cell-mate called Renza, not long back — recollect?'

Joe snorted. 'That slimy sonuver! I never lost no sleep when someone finally knifed him. Woulda sold out his own mother for two-bits. His brain was pickled in booze.'

'More likely that liquid manure you brew up in the cells from potato peelings and rotten fruit,' growled Bascombe. Joe looked mighty wary now, licked his lips.

'Renza's enemies finally caught up with him in the breakfast queue,' Santee went on. 'Four-inch spike hammered right through his chest. He was scared of dying, wanted to put a lot of things *straight* he reckoned. Babbled like a crazy man, took us a while to figure out what he was saying. One thing he kept coming back to was when you went loco on that firewater — you broke down, crying, told him a crazy story about seeing a murder on a river sandbank, while you fought off a naked woman!'

Bascombe shook his head, laughing scornfully. 'Sounds like a dirty-old man's wishful thinkin', Joe!'

Navajo Joe's eyes bulged as he stared back. His mouth worked but nothing intelligible came out for a minute or two, only spittle.

'You convinced Renza you were there, Joe,' snapped the sheriff. 'On the other side of the river, havin' your eyes scratched out by this naked woman!' The lawman snorted. 'Mind, I can savvy any woman wantin' to scratch out your eyes, you got close to her. You have ta go Injun when you want a woman, don't you, Joe? White girls won't come within spittin' distance of you.'

Scars around Joe's eyes showed white through the dirt. He blinked. Then his filthy face hardened: he'd been insulted, and briefly there was a flare of defiance in the rheumy eyes.

'It were no dream! She was real! A wildcat! She near ripped my eyes outa my head — then she ran. But they shot her hoss, and, buck-nekked like she was, stumblin', stones hurtin' her feet — she never stood a chance!'

Joe stopped abruptly, realising, too late, that he had let the sheriff's taunting get to him and now he had said too much. The guard curled a lip, obviously still sceptical.

Santee pushed off the wall. 'What does that mean — 'Didn't stand a chance'? Did they catch her? They kill her? *What*, damn you.'

Joe seemed to shrink inside himself. 'They got her — Wha-whatever you can think of, they done it to her.' He looked around wildly, gripping the edge of the desk until his knuckles were white. 'It was . . . awful. This little runt runnin' round, screamin' 'Do this! Do that!' Urgin' on the others . . . 'specially the big one with white hair. They all seemed to be pushin' him around . . . aw, look, I need a drink.'

'You need to answer a helluva lot more questions, Joe, that's what you need.' Santee's voice was hard now, his bleak gaze causing a tic to start jumping in Joe's face under his left eye.

'Look, I had nothin' to do with it!' Joe's cracked voice lifted and his breathing filled the small room like the sluggish panting of a locomotive at a siding.

'You were there!' snapped the sheriff. 'You've gone too far to back off now — and you try to give us the runaround I'll see to it you die in here, Joe. No marker on your grave, just a hole in the mud on the river-bank.'

Santee frowned slightly as Navajo Joe reared back, his mouth working, fear-filled eyes swivelling towards Santee. He started to lift a hand in some kind of gesture of appeal but let it drop to his side. 'What . . . you want me to say?'

The sheriff's gaze didn't soften or waver. 'Whatever you feel you ought to tell us, Joe, but it'd better be what we want to hear.'

The lawman glanced at Santee, lips pulled into a mirthless smile. He winked, but it was merely the movement of an eyelid, without meaning.

Santee seemed mildly baffled but gave his attention to Joe. 'What were you doing at the river in the first place?'

'I'd come down outa the hills.' Joe's voice sounded defeated and his gaze kept swivelling towards the lawman. 'I'd been prospectin', but had no luck, so I lit-out. Lost my pack-mule off a high trail an' had to slog it on foot.'

Bascombe leaned closer, cut in harshly, 'You were on the run, 'cause you jumped Salty O'Hare's claim! Near killed him an' stole his cache of silver.'

'No! I was set-up! They never found no silver on me.'

The sheriff smiled crookedly. 'Mebbe because it was in the packs on that mule you lost over the cliff.'

Navajo looked worried then, started to speak, and took a deep breath,

15

continuing, 'I got down outa the hills on foot and made for the river. Seen a hoss grazin', not even ground-hitched, and some female clothin' hangin' on the bushes.'

'So you went an' got yourself an eyeful!' the sheriff said contemptuously.

'I might be old, but I ain't dead!'

'What'd you do to her to make her want to scratch your eyes out?' Santee asked quietly.

'Nothin'! I swear! I only grabbed her arm an' . . . then there was shoutin' on t'other side of the river. Couldn't see a lot 'cause of the bushes, but I heard a shot and then she went for my eyes, broke away and started to run. I couldn't see and I fell into the water.'

'First bath he's had in years!' opined the prison guard, but only got cold looks by way of reaction.

'I can't swim an' I kinda panicked, hauled myself up under low-hangin' bushes in the shallows. Then there was more gunfire an' they shot her horse.' He paused, looking at Santee and then the sheriff. 'Well, it was hard to see clearly, just hazy things movin'. When I heard 'em comin' across the river I lay doggo, worked way back under the brush overhang. She musta been runnin' for her life by then. Someone yelled, 'Don't shoot her!' and not long after I hears her screamin' — I-I could see a mite better by then.'

'Tell us what you saw, Joe,' Santee urged quietly.

'They had her back on the sandbar where they'd killed that ranny — I din' know 'twas Josh Rankin then — they done some awful things to her.'

'Could you identify these men?'

'No! Never!' Joe shook his head emphatically, licking his lips as he stared at the sheriff. 'Couldn't see all that good. Fact, din' want to, the way she was screamin'. Then it just stopped. But I can still hear her screamin', in the middle of the night, sometimes even durin' the day.'

Joe was shaking almost crying.

'How many were there?'

'Three — mebbe four, coulda been five. Was all mixed up — just shadows. A tall feller with white hair, that little runt, others, just . . . men. They threw her in the river! I was upstream so she never drifted my way. Not long after that, they took off.'

'Leaving the dead man?'

Navajo Joe nodded. 'See, Sher'ff? I can't help you. I couldn't identify any of 'em. Never seen a single one clearly. Hell, I pissed myself I was so scared they was gonna find me. I lay doggo till dark, then got outa there fast.'

The sheriff made a couple of notes. 'And you told no one about this?'

'No one, Sher'ff! I swear! Not a livin' soul.'

'Except Renza,' Santee said.

'Aw, I din' know what I was doin' then. Whole thing'd been preyin' on my mind and that rotgut loosened my tongue.' Tears smeared his dirty cheeks now. 'That gal, she weren't very old, a real looker. Not right she died that way.'

'Put away the violins, Joe!' growled

the sheriff. 'Now this was a coupla weeks ago. Senator Rankin raised hell when he found out it was his son was murdered on that sandbar.' The lawman leaned across the table and back-handed Joe across the mouth. 'C'mon, Joe!'

'Stop that,' Santee said, in his quiet drawl and he and the lawman locked gazes while Joe groaned, dabbing at his bleeding lips. The sheriff sat back in his chair, shrugging, as he spoke again to the prisoner.

'You knew what'd happened and you didn't come forward! Not even when the senator offered a reward for information about his son's murder! Don't sound like you, Joe. Who the hell you tryin' to fool?'

'I-I was mighty scared! I was already in jail by then, waitin' for trial 'cause of that trumped-up claim-jumpin' charge, and — well, I figured once I'd spoke out, them fellers who were on that sandbank would know I'd seen 'em. An' they'd get to me, in jail or not.' He stopped, furtive and more scared than ever. Joe looked at Santee and there was a plea on his filthy face and in his shaky voice. 'They'd never let me live to testify, not them cold-blooded killers, so I kept mum.'

Santee nodded slowly in understanding but the sheriff growled.

'Sounds to me like mebbe you could identify 'em. Knew just who might come after you.'

'No, Sher'ff! I swear on my mother's life!'

'Scum like you don't have mothers, Joe — they just pick somethin' outa the pig swill an' rear it!'

Santee said flatly, again locking gazes with the sheriff, 'Cut it out, Bascombe. That sort of thing gets us nowhere. You go through her saddle-bags before you took off, Joe?'

Joe jerked his head up, not expecting that question. He swallowed, nodded slowly. 'I was hungry, broke. I never found nothin' I could use, just small change — an' female stuff. Clothes, face paint, a cheap necklace thing with a broken chain, kinda cat's head on it — meant to be laughin', I guess. Not worth anythin'.'

'Notice the brand on the horse?'

Bascombe blinked as he looked sharply at Santee. Joe frowned. 'Well, din' take much notice. Think it mighta been a triangle with a couple Xs in it.'

Santee glanced at the sheriff. 'Know it?'

Bascombe shook his head. 'No spread in my bailiwick with that brand.'

'How about a livery? She might've hired the horse.'

Bascombe blew out his cheeks, shook his head. Joe said nothing, stiffened slightly when Santee turned his gaze on him.

'You've helped some, Joe. You think of anything more, you let me know. I'll see what I can do about getting a little time off your sentence.'

The sheriff stood, eyes narrowed. 'I never heard you was soft in the head, Santee.'

'There's a lot you haven't heard about me, Bascombe.'

'Well, don't reckon I'll hear about you doin' much on this, Joe din' tell us anythin' we couldn't figure for ourselves.'

'We got a couple of things.'

The sheriff arched his eyebrows. 'What, for hell's sake?'

'Big man with fair hair, a loudmouthed runt urging everyone to commit mayhem — the girl's body has never been found, either, far as we know.'

'Judas! What're you gettin' all fussed for? That'd tell you nothin', even if she did turn up!'

'Not if she's dead. But what if she made it out of that river alive . . . ?'

'You're loco, Santee! Joe said they killed her. You're grabbin' at straws.'

Santee was very sober. 'If straws are all I've got, then I'll grab at 'em. Before you go, Joe, what'd she look like, this naked wildcat of yours?'

Joe's seamed old face softened. 'Aw,

she was a looker. Young, like I said, lots of dark hair, grey eyes that sorta stood out against her skin which was kinda gold — mebbe a Mex. Funny li'l nose, sort of a turn-up on the tip, and her mouth . . . ' He paused, swallowing. 'Aw, it was a damn shame what happened to her. Feel sick to my stomach every time I think about it.'

'How tall?' Santee asked, ignoring Bascombe who was trying to tell Bale to take Joe away.

'Tall? She come to my shoulder — an' slim. Them grey eyes of hers were cold as ice when she clawed me. She was a real hellcat when she was steamin', usin' knees, elbows, teeth . . . ' He let it fade away, drew a deep breath.

They waited, but Joe was all through and Bascombe jerked his head at the guard. Bale shuffled forward and took Navajo Joe by one skinny arm, leading him out. The old prospector was shaking like a leaf in a high wind, feet dragging.

'What's your part in this, Santee? I

know you work for the governor, but — what d'you actually do?'

'I'm his troubleshooter.' Santee spoke in clipped tones, obviously not wanting any more questions. He hitched up his belt, straightened his trail-worn hat and started for the door. 'Thanks for your help, Bascombe.' He paused with his hand on the door knob. 'One thing: they told me the warden here's your brother, but his name's Waters.'

'Half-brother — we get along OK.' The sheriff smiled thinly, aware Santee was just trying to forestall further questions about his interest in this and his obvious discomfort. But the lawman wasn't about to let it go. 'That trouble-shootin' — it include bodyguardin'? Say, for the governor, or his friends?'

Santee's face was skull-tight. 'Sometimes.'

The sheriff smiled and leaned back in his chair, hands folded just under his belt.

'Uh-huh.' Bascombe grinned tightly,

ignoring Santee's dangerous look. 'Think I savvy now why you're so fired-up and flim-flammed about this.' The crooked smile widened and there was a deal of satisfaction in the lawman's voice as he added, 'You was s'posed to be guardin' Josh Rankin, wasn't you?'

2

Santee

He rarely used his first name — Jim — so most folk knew him simply as Santee. With his mahogany skin and dark hair he looked part-Indian except for those grey eyes, which contrasted startlingly with his leather-look hide.

But he was no more Indian than Wallace Burdin, Governor of Arizona Territory: there were still folk who would never allow any man who had even a faint touch of Indian in his blood to hold the governorship. But Burdin was OK — he could trace his ancestors back to Merrie Olde England if he had to — and he had had to do just that before he was appointed to his present position.

Santee didn't know his birth name: he was captured as a child, less than two years old, by the Santee Sioux raiding party that massacred the wagon-train his parents had been travelling with. He was reared by the Indians until he was 'rescued' by a cavalry patrol and reluctantly returned to the white man's world almost ten years later.

It took a heap of living-down his origins, once they became known. At first he had done his best to hide them, but kids being kids, he had been taunted about his sun-dark skin and his stilted, halting English, plus some Indian ways he hadn't yet managed to shake. Fights had been frequent and he soon learned that he could beat most opponents by using Indian-style wrestling grips and flying leaps ending with hard-soled feet invariably knocking out his challengers. But parents quickly tired of that — some boys had huge dental bills, others had damaged hearing, fractured bones or broken noses.

Santee was summarily punished, by a

group of fathers, brothers and other kin of his vanquished opponents. Mostly grown men, five of them, plus three teenage boys, encircled him and beat him with their fists and boots. They left him broken and bleeding and when he eventually managed to stagger back to the Boys Home he found his meagre belongings scattered around the front lawn and the door locked.

Hurt in more ways than just the physical injuries, he collected what was left of his things and crept away into the night.

A long time later, and a long way from the home, an old widow found him stealing her shucked corn in her barn one winter night. She took pity on him, dropped the switch she carried and took him into her house, fed and clothed him. Her kindness saved a lot of lives, because even at that tender age of around twelve or fourteen — Santee could never be accurate about his age — he had intended to kill the men who had beaten him. It took a lot to talk him out of it but Widow McPherson managed to do it, with her warm Scots brogue eventually reaching through to him. The problem was he still thought like an Indian. She taught him many things, to help ease him into the ways of white people in whose world he now had to live. After a while she even showed him how to use a gun — a rifle. She had had to hunt meat for herself for over twenty years of widowhood and she was a good shot. She also had a neighbour who came once in a while and helped her out with the heavier chores — chopping wood for the winter, deepening the well, building and swinging a new barn door, replacing shingles blown off in the bitter winds: all chores she was capable of doing herself, and had on plenty of occasions. But the neighbour, known only as Rimfire, was on a self-imposed penance, felt a strong need to help folk after years of riding the owlhoot trail, killing for money: he was that rarity of the Old West, a conscience-stricken retired gunfighter. He saw a lot of himself in his early years in Jim Santee, had a hunch this youth was headed for a violent life and, after a lot of thought, sensing innate goodness in Santee, he decided to teach him all he knew about handling a six-shooter — with a simple, earnest warning.

'You ever abuse what I'm showin' you, boy, an' I'll strap on that old hogleg of mine and I'll find you — and I promise you, all you can expect of such a meetin' will be a wooden marker on the nearest boothill.'

Santee was an apt pupil and stayed with the widow for six years, until she died of a heart attack while fighting off a horse-thief in her corrals one time while Santee was absent.

That thief was the first man Santee killed — with Rimfire's full approval. Jim tracked the thief for seven weeks, finally cornered him in a saloon. The man had laughed in his face when he came for him.

'Kid, you want to grow into a man,

turn round right now and get outa here, otherwise, I swear I'll shoot to kill, you make me go for my gun.'

'Go for it, and see if I care, you murderin' snake!' Santee snapped and went for his own Colt.

Surprised, the horse-thief died where he stood against the bar, gun only half-drawn, a bullet through the centre of his chest. When he fell to the filthy, sawdusted floor, the barkeep, recovering, said, 'Kid, you better get outa here. Our sheriff won't give you no break just because you're young . . . an' he don't like 'breeds.'

Santee took the advice but the sheriff headed-up a small posse anyway and eventually ran him down in a dry gulch.

''Kid, we can shoot you full of holes between draws on our cigarettes, if we want. You give up and I'll treat you right. You done what you figured you had to, but you gotta learn the white man's ways, respect his laws.'

Santee didn't like that white man crack, but with six rifles and a sawn-off shotgun trained on him he had little choice but to surrender.

The sheriff's way of 'seeing him right' was to beat the living daylights out of him three days in a row, then put him on a chaingang, building a road through the mountains for the stageline that was coming through there before spring. He was known as Kid Santee amongst the other prisoners and the guards, and they all considered him to be jinxed, a kid who attracted trouble like dung attracted flies.

So he was shunned, but that suited him. He was essentially a loner and in his solitude, he worked out a way to escape. No one had ever done it before, and none who knew about it gave him any chance of success. But he did it, even managed to bend a gun barrel over the head of the traitorous sheriff, before taking off and losing himself in the savage wilderness of the mountains. There were advantages to being part-Indian — if not in blood, sure in knowledge learned from ten years amongst the Santees, the only people who had been part of his world at that time.

Easily shaking the searchers, he headed west and south, and with the learned gun-lore added to his Indian background, and the bitter experience of the chain-gang, he had a powerful urge to see what lay over the next horizon. And the next — and the one after that. *He didn't know just what he was looking for, but he sure was looking* . . .

So Santee was suddenly loose in an unsuspecting world. His trails were long and often violent; the years were not always kind: men died by his guns, and other men's bullets sometimes found resting places in his lean body. With several bounties on his head, he at last found refuge in the Confederate States Army where the war made him untouchable.

And afterwards, few remembered Kid Santee — he had made sergeant because of his talent for fighting and his wilderness knowledge. The army insisted on a first name and he had settled on Jim, borrowing it from Widow McPherson's long-dead husband. So in his postwar wanderings he became Jim Santee or just plain Santee. There were ranch jobs and trail herds, bad companions and good, once even a short stint as a deputy lawman in Wichita.

And there were gunfights. He walked away from most, was carried away from several, but he was still alive, even if he had been given up for dead by doctors on two occasions, he had fought through, despite all misgivings and doleful predictions.

He drifted aimlessly, mostly content. Then he found a job he enjoyed: riding shotgun for the Overland Stage Line. He tangled with robbers and troublesome passengers, handled it all with enthusiasm and competence. Once he held off two Mexicans and three American outlaws for over a day, alone, in the northern New Mexico desert. The driver and the only armed passenger lay dead on the burning sand. The remaining three passengers were two women, one mature, the other not yet out of her teens, and a young drummer who showed no inclination to fight. Santee was left to hold off the outlaws. He killed one and thought he wounded another, forcing them into retreat.

The four survivors saw him as the only obstacle between them and the strongbox now, and, impatient, they charged the crippled stagecoach.

That was their mistake: Santee had been in a very similar situation during the war, the only survivor against a Yankee patrol which wanted secret military papers in a valise chained to the wrist of the newly dead lieutenant, sprawled at Santee's feet.

Santee had killed them all in a savage shoot-out and almost died of his wounds. They gave him a medal afterwards, but he later threw it away.

This time the four robbers came in from different sides as they made their attack on the stage. Santee had half-expected such a move and rolled beneath the canted vehicle: one rear wheel had been shattered by the thieves in order to stop the stage. He used his own and the dead driver's shotguns. Buckshot cut down the two Mexicans in their tracks but then there were no more shells for the shotguns. Santee dropped the weapons, rolled out from under and ran behind the coach before the two remaining men lifted their heads. When they did, he killed one, but the other ducked. For what seemed like hours, there was no more shooting from the lone robber, and the passengers pleaded with Santee to allow them out of the stifling, uncomfortable coach.

'Stay put! That skunk's lying low!' snapped Santee.

But the drummer, showing off to the young woman, Santee suspected, stepped out, spreading his arms, saying, 'See? You either scared him off or nailed him, mister. You can relax now, you done a fine job. Don't you think so, Miz Bur — ?'

The gunshot drowned the last word and the young man staggered, eyes wide in surprise, blood spilling from his mouth as the bullet in his back slammed him forward.

'Stay down, ladies!' yelled Santee.

They only knew he was behind the coach, didn't know what he was doing. But he had crept to the front where the team was trapped by the traces having been caught up on the steeply angled vehicle. He crawled over the dead driver and slashed the knotted leather with his hunting knife, freeing it from where it had been jammed.

The struggling team lurched up with various whinnies and neighs and started to run. Santee grabbed at a trailing rein with his left hand, was jerked violently off his feet.

The horses ran on, and he ploughed through the desert sand, body twisting, right hand gripping his Colt which held his last two cartridges. The robber was crouched behind a dune and jumped into view, startled, when the team came thundering over the crest with Santee being dragged behind a bow-wave of sand. He lifted his gun, firing wildly, and Santee released the leather, rolling aside as sand erupted twice near his moving body. Then, still rolling, he felt a searing thump low down in his side.

Gritting his teeth, he dug in with his heels and knees, the movement having a braking effect that jerked him half upright. The outlaw, bewildered, fumbled to steady his footing and bring up his gun. Santee's two bullets took him down, throwing him violently across the slope . . .

'Miss Bur — ' turned out to be Miss Deborah Burdin, sister of Governor-elect Wallace Burdin, on her way to be at her brother's side during his inauguration.

Recovering from the bullet wound in his side incurred during the defence of the stage, Santee was surprised to see Wallace Burdin with Deborah and a small retinue coming into the infirmary where he was propped up in bed.

Burdin, a large man in his early forties, features a little too heavy, but with a smile that set the ladies' hearts all a'flutter, turned on the charm as he walked straight to Santee's bedside, hand outstreched.

'Wallace Burdin, Mr Santee, Governor-elect.' It was one of the very few times anyone had used a Mister in front of his name and Santee seemed a mite dazed as he shook hands.

'Jim Santee, Governor.'

'Fine — Jim it is, though not quite Governor yet — inauguration's a week or so away. You know my sister, Deborah, here, and I have to say she has painted a glowing picture of your fight with those stage robbers.'

Santee looked up carefully as the man let his words trail off. 'Just doing what I was paid to do, Governor.'

'You hear that, folks? Genuine modesty! Now if a couple of my team would only take a leaf out of Mr Santee's book . . . ?' He laughed as his companions shuffled a trifle awkwardly but smiled dutifully.

'Not bein' modest,' broke in Santee frowning in annoyance. 'Just that there was no one else to do it. If they'd gotten past me — '

'Exactly, Mr Santee!' cut in Burdin, his smile fading. 'If those men had won the day — well, I hate to even contemplate such a situation!' He slid an arm about his sister's shoulders. She had gone pale, shivering slightly. 'You saved my sister from the Lord knows what kind of fate, Mr Santee. You should, and will, be rewarded.'

'Governor, the Overland Company has already offered me a cash appreciation — '

'And I hear you have asked that it be given to the local Indian Reservation . . . ?'

Santee's frown deepened, saw they were waiting for an answer. 'I was raised by Santee Sioux. Years after the cavalry rescued me I went back to see my Indian family. Why the hell them deadheads in Washington can't just leave Indians to their own way of life I just don't savvy! They was much better off — and happier — living the old way. Well, I ain't going to go into the squalor and misery side of it now, but I've glimpsed that reservation in the hills back yonder, on Little Mountain, and it don't look any better than the Sioux had. I don't need that money. But the Indian Agent better be honest or he's gonna get a visit from me he'll long remember!'

There was silence in the infirmary and then Wallace Burdin said, quite soberly, looking around at his group, 'Folks, if this isn't the man to have at my side while I'm governor, then I don't know who is! Ladies and gents, I give you my new bodyguard and trouble-shooter — Mr Jim Santee!'

$\star$ $\star$ $\star$

Santee thought about the offer to be the new governor's trouble-shooter, body-guard and general protector. The bullet wound was a little more serious than the doctor had at first thought and he would need a longer recuperation than originally predicted.

Burdin or Miss Deborah came to see him two or three times as the days passed, waiting on his decision, but never hurrying him. He had his own ways of finding out that Wallace Burdin was a man who lived up to his promises and had a good wide streak of compassion in him: truly a man of the people. He was eager to lift Arizona from a territory to statehood.[1]

Santee accepted the job and was good at it. Only twice did he have to use his gun to defend the governor from fanatical enemies, but, sometimes without Burdin ever knowing his life

---

[1] Burdin would not see this latter come to pass in his lifetime, but he did set the wheels rolling smoothly for Congress to eventually grant full statehood to Arizona Territory although not until 1912.

had been in jeopardy, Santee's fists had ensured the governor's safety and that of Miss Deborah. Once he had rescued her from would-be kidnappers and the governor realized just what an asset he had in this Indian-raised protector. Santee enjoyed a good life, especially after Miss Deborah finally got over her schoolgirl crush on him and found herself a real love: Josh Rankin, youngest son of a California senator who had a lot of dealings with Burdin.

Twice Santee accompanied her as a bodyguard when she went to visit the Rankins' extensive vineyards in California. Once he had to intervene when she was riding, lost herself in brush, and found herself facing two bearded drifters with lascivious eyes. Under a cocked gun, Santee had taken the girl back to safety, then went back looking for the drifters — and found them.

It was unlikely any other female would be threatened by them . . .

The senator was impressed, arranged with Burdin to borrow Santee while he travelled on a campaign trail for a local election and was in need of sound protection.

It was a success, Santee settling several nasty episodes, without bringing undue attention to the senator. Burdin's own team occasionally used his services after that. He didn't mind — it was boring most of the time with Burdin, now he was safely ensconced in the governor's seat at Prescott — and Santee enjoyed the travel and occasional action.

The term 'trouble-shooter' didn't live up to its name with Burdin: the man was a rarity, an *honest* politician who seemed to be uninterested in merely lining his own pocket. He came from a well-established family and probably had no need for the proceeds of graft. He also seemed to find an easy rapport with the Arizonans and listened to what they wanted. If it was practical and of some benefit to the Territory, he gave it to them — even if what they were given wasn't *exactly* what they had in mind.

But he had the knack of tactfully convincing them with his persuasive rhetoric that 'it' was best for everyone.

Miss Deborah's wedding was coming up in another couple of months and Josh Rankin, destined to run his father's large cattle estates outside of California, was to go visit several ranches, selecting and buying the best breeding stock before the big day. He was young, barely twenty, and had been brought up in West Coast colleges and boarding-schools. His outlook on life was necessarily boyish. He enjoyed pranks and jokes, and could take both when turned upon him. But he displayed a natural bargaining power and an innate sense of just how good was an animal being offered to him.

Of course, Senator Rankin asked that Santee accompany Josh as bodyguard, for at certain times the young Rankin would be carrying or collecting large sums of money. And his high spirits occasionally made him reckless.

Santee was looking forward to the

job: it promised variety, possibly a little action, and young Josh was good company, if a mite boisterous after a few drinks. But, essentially, he was a good-natured drunk and Santee saw he didn't have too many hangovers. Deborah had wanted to go, but there were several functions the governor needed to either attend or arrange and so she stayed behind to act as official hostess, seeing as the governor was a widower.

Josh and Santee began their long journey through the cattle ranches.

The first few weeks went smoothly and then they headed into wilder country, with many lonely miles between spreads. Finding reliable men to drive the purchased stock back to the collection point at Tucson became harder and Santee wasn't happy with a few of the choices Josh made.

But the young man was determined to do his best for his father so Santee held his peace. When he made a bad choice he blamed no one but himself, and Santee liked this about him — he took steps to settle it himself. Only once did he have to intervene and side Josh in a shoot-out: the boy caught his first bullet wound. Only a burn, really, across the ribs, but it was enough to remind the lad he was mortal.

They got on well together, Josh Rankin and Santee.

Then everything went wrong: everything.

3

No Witnesses

Santee could smell the whiskey on the warden's breath across the wide desk as he settled into the visitor's chair. Laird Waters stared at him suspiciously, folding his hands in his lap in an effort to shield their trembling: it was almost time for another snort of the top-brand hooch half-brother Walt Bascombe kept him supplied with.

He'd get rid of this pesky 'breed, or whateverthehell he was, quickly, and fill a tumbler to the brim . . .

'B'lieve you were here with my brother just t'other day, Santee.'

'That's right, Warden. Interviewing a prisoner named Navajo Joe.'

Waters frowned. 'Navajo — ? Din' know we had any damn 'breeds in our community.' A crooked, unrepentant smile moved his thin lips. 'Your presence excepted, o'course.'

'I'm neither half-breed, nor a member of your so called community, Warden. Joe was in the gang building that new rock wall above the river.'

Suddenly Warden Laird Waters was worried. He sat up, ran a tongue across his lips, let his gaze slide to a small cabinet at shoulder level within reach of his chair.

'Go on — have your snort,' Santee told him and the man snapped his head around.

'You trying to be funny?'

Santee shrugged. 'An early morning snifter sometimes works wonders.'

Waters stared, then smiled thinly. 'So I hear. And damn! Just might put it to the test!'

'Thought you might.'

Waters got up quickly and went to the cupboard, brought out a labelled bottle, still with its tissue paper wrapping, though it had been torn away from the neck. He held it where Santee could see it was almost two-thirds full.

'Genuine bourbon, all the way from Kentucky — Walt treats me good.' He more than half-filled a large glass, quickly drank some and topped up the level as he smacked his lips. He looked sidelong at Santee as he slapped the stopper back into the neck. 'Sorry, just enough for me here.'

'Doubt that, Warden.' Santee gestured to a shelf he could see with three other tissue-wrapped bottles on it. 'But you got enough back-up there to see you through the week.'

Waters pinched down his eyes, slammed the cupboard doors and dropped into his chair, drinking again from his glass. Santee could see the mellowness coming back with a rush. 'Navajo Joe, huh?' He shook his large head, ran a hand across his thinning hair. 'You can't see him.'

'Warden, do I have to remind you I'm working for the governor on this?'

'Hell, I know who you are, Santeee. Most folk've heard of you and how tough you think you are. Don't cut nothin' with me — you still can't see Navajo Joe.'

'I hope you've got a good reason.'

Waters laughed and drained his glass, slapping it down noisily on the edge of his desk. He hunched his shoulders as he leaned forward. 'I have The best — very *best*!'

'Let's hear it.'

'And so you shall. Just a minute.' He went to the cupboard and poured himself another half-tumbler of whiskey, sat down and gulped some. His mean eyes were glinting now. 'You can't see Joe . . . because he's dead.'

Santee stiffened: that had been the last thing he had expected. 'Not two days since I saw him — and he was in tolerable shape then, considering this hell-hole — now he's dead?'

'As the beefsteak I've ordered for my supper.'

Santee's face set in hard lines as he leaned forward. Waters eased back warily. '*How*?' Santee barked.

The warden jumped slightly, steadied himself down with another gulp of whiskey. 'Fell off the wall we got 'em buildin'. Couldn't swim, poor feller. Anyway, he'd bounced off a few rocks before he hit the water they tell me.'

'Did he slip? Have a fight?'

'*Hell, no!* Damn you, Santee, don't you go stirring up a hornets' nest where there ain't any! It was a plumb unfortunate accident. Plenty of witnesses to swear to that.'

Santee held the man's gaze until he looked away. 'Can I speak with the guard who was on duty at the time?'

Waters was already shaking his head before Santee had finished. 'You're outa luck. He was due for some leave. I approved a coupla weeks. He's a good worker, does what he's told, no hassles, like some of 'em. He's earned a break.'

Santee kept his steady gaze on Waters' face and the man's hand trembled some this time when he took another drink. 'Don't suppose he went anywhere close by for his vacation?'

Waters shrugged. 'Dunno, exactly. Recollect he talked about Nevada or Oregon a few times. Maybe got kin up that way.' The warden was mighty mellow now, happy with the way he was handling things.

Santee nodded slowly, stood. 'Thanks, Warden. I'll see myself out.'

'Sure thing — anythin' else I can help you with just say the word.'

Hand on the office doorknob, Santee spoke over his shoulder. 'What was the guard's name? Wouldn't be Bale, would it?'

Waters' smiled faded a trifle. 'How — how'd you know that, for God's sake?'

'Lucky guess.'

★ ★ ★

Sheriff Walt Bascombe wasn't pleased to see Santee walk into his office, and didn't trouble to hide the fact.

'Judas priest! You still in town?'

'You need eyeglasses, Bascombe,' Santee said, toeing out a straight back chair and dropping into it. He thumbed back his hat, looking steadily across the cluttered desk at the sheriff.

'Why the hell you say that?'

Santee spread his arms as if saying 'Here I am'.

Bascombe scowled. 'Ah, smart-ass, huh?'

'Smarter than your stupid question.'

Bascombe, who had been standing, eased himself into his chair, frowning, watching Santee closely. 'What's the burr under your saddle? I've co-operated with you since you arrived in town. What more d'you want?'

Santee took out his tobacco sack and papers and began building a cigarette. He sighed. 'Aw, just edgy, I guess. I wanted to ask Navajo Joe a couple things, but your brother tells me he's dead.'

'Yeah — fell off the wall an' drowned. Day after we'd seen him. No, I tell a lie — was the same afternoon, just after we left. I've looked into it. Just an accident.'

Santee lit up, shook out the match flame slowly. 'But quick.'

'What d'you mean *quick*?'

'Someone closed Joe's mouth for him mighty fast after I'd questioned him . . . Just like he'd mebbe said a mite too much and they didn't want him expanding on it.'

Bascombe's eyes narrowed. 'You tread easy, Santee.'

'Why, Sheriff? Something I said bothering you?'

'No — an' I don't aim to let anything you say bother me. So, you can stop wastin' your time and mine.'

'Hmmm — never looked at it that way . . . That guard we had in the office with Joe, he's missing, too.'

'Bale's on leave, is all.'

'Uh-huh. Your brother hinted at Nevada or Oregon. Like to bet on when — if ever — he comes back?'

'Just what the hell you tryin' to say, Santee? No, c'mon, spit it out. You're tellin' me somethin', but I want to hear it in plain language.'

Santee took two drags on his cigarette before answering, those steel-grey eyes making the sheriff look away while he searched for a match to light the cheroot he took from his pocket. Santee snapped a vesta into flame and held it for the lawman. Bascombe looked up through the clouds of smoke, blinking.

'Best tread careful, mister.'

'Warrior named Raven Fast-eye taught me that before I even knew how to speak his lingo properly.'

'Mebbe you shoulda stayed with him. We're talkin' white man lingo now, Santee, you best remember that. You might work for the governor but you're in my bailiwick now and I'm a kind of governor here — folk listen when I speak, do what I say — if they know what's good for 'em.'

Santee nodded. 'I've noticed. If Bale was here I guess he'd agree with that, too.'

Bascombe stood abruptly. 'Damn you for a lousy 'breed! Look, get outa my

56

office. No! Get right outa my town. Judas, a man tries to help you and you come in makin' all kindsa accusations.'

'Name one.'

Bascombe blinked. 'What . . . ?'

'What've I accused you of? C'mon, Walt, tell me.'

The sheriff's face was murderous. He swung suddenly to a rack right beside the desk and snatched a sawn-off shotgun, spinning back towards Santee, then froze — staring into the muzzle of the man's Colt, the hammer back at full cock.

Judas priest! Still sitting down and drew that fast!

'You don't want to use that, Walt. 'Fact, you can't. I see your knuckle whiten and I'll blow you out from under your hat . . . Now, set it down gently on the rack again — that's it.'

'You *better* quit town!' Bascombe gritted.

'Yeah, reckon I agree with you there — but you'll see me again, Walt. You and the white-haired son of a bitch and whoever else was with you on that sandbank.'

'Why-w-*what* . . . ? You're loco! I never . . .'

Bascombe sat down quickly because his legs simply wouldn't hold him upright any longer, his face greyish.

Santee nodded curtly and left, tossing over his wide shoulder,

'*Hasta la vista*, Walt.'

★　★　★

He went to the general store and bought some staples for the trail. Before he had visited Bascombe, he had sent off a telegraph message to Sandy Scully, head of the Governor's Campaign Office. Here there was massive research available through contacts all over the country, even in some widespread parts of the civilized world if need be — so that in any important speech or letter or submission to Washington, Wallace Burdin had his facts right.

Scully had had his orders ever since Santee had started working for the governor to give the bodyguard any — any — assistance he required. And promptly.

Santee had wired a description of the brand on the black horse that had belonged to the mystery woman and been shot dead as she was trying to flee the murder scene at the river. On his way to collect his own mount from the livery, he called into the telegraph office, but there was no reply yet.

'I'll go have some supper and maybe stop by again,' Santee told the operator. 'You open for a spell yet?'

'Just till seven.'

'OK — if there's no reply, means it won't come in till tomorrow. Forward it on to Jim Santee, General Delivery, Painted Rock.'

'Ain't no telegraph office at Painted Rock.'

'All right. You tell me where, somewhere in the Painted Rock direction.'

'Gila Bend's got one at the railroad depot.'

'Use that.'

The man, Arch Thomas, was in his late fifties, mighty short of hair, but what was there stuck out in twists of grey. His eyes had bags under them and he had coughed several times. He stared levelly at Santee, not moving or answering. Jim sighed, and dug out two silver dollars, laying them on the counter with a snapping sound.

'That wire better be at the depot when I check.'

The operator smiled now, showing mostly gums, as he scooped the coins dexterously into his shirt pocket. 'You can count on me, Mr Santee, guarantee it.'

Santee nodded and gave Thomas a half smile before leaving. 'Sounds good.'

Outside, he was surprised to see how dark it was getting, and, still carrying his gunnysack of supplies from the general store, made his way by a back lane to Prickett Square where he knew there was a diner that served palatable food.

He ate unhurriedly, had a second cup of coffee and smoked a cigarette before picking up his gunnysack and leaving. On the boardwalk he stopped to have a last drag on his smoke, then flicked the butt into the gutter. The streets were busy, quite a few cowboys starting to get rowdy enough for some people to cross the street to dodge them. He decided he might as well check with the telegraph office one more time then go back and see if the hotel room he had earlier cancelled, was available for one more night. He would leave in daylight and head upriver to where Josh Rankin's brutal murder took place.

He turned into the back lane he had used to come to the square, carrying the gunnysack casually over his left shoulder. He smiled faintly, recollecting the way Sheriff Bascombe had almost come apart when he had thrown in that bit about men being there *with him* on the sandbar. It was meant just as a niggling thing, because he sensed that Bascombe knew more than he was telling, but he hadn't quite expected the reaction he provoked.

Maybe he would look in on the sheriff again before he quit this depressing town . . .

Afterwards he blamed himself: mooching along in the unlit lane, musing over things, when he ought to have been watching the shadows.

At first, there were only two of them, but later there had been a third man present, though he hadn't seen him clearly. The first two chose the darkest patch in the lane like the pros they were, one coming at him from each side.

His Indian-trained senses were working but just a fraction too late. A fist slammed into his right kidney but as he had been starting to turn into a less dark patch it only grazed him instead of driving all the way home. He staggered though, into the punch swung at his head by the second man. But his stumble took him too close and the fist skidded along his jaw and over his shoulder, failing to connect solidly. The gunnysack, with its hefty load of grub and a spare carton of cartridges, crashed against the side of the puncher's head and knocked him back against the clapboard wall of a building, grunting.

Santee dropped to one knee, back afire and slowing him a mite, and the first man's kick skidded across his spine. He fell full length, rolled towards the man, using his moving weight against his shins to send him off-balance. By then Santee was coming up, swinging the gunnysack again. It hit hard — there were cans of beans in there — and the stumbling attacker flew back across the lane, going down, arms flailing.

The other one came in swinging and Santee had to drop the sack, get his arms up to parry the blows. He was only partially successful, felt his jaw jar and a lip split. He ducked under the next swing, snapped the top of his head up under the other's jaw. He grabbed a sweaty shirtfront as the man stepped back, pulled him in sharply and lifted a knee into his crotch. There was a sick grunt and hands clawed at him weakly. He knocked them aside, brought up the knee again — this time into the down-dropping face as the man doubled over.

He was still falling when Santee swung at a sound behind him, hand reaching for his six-gun — but the holster was empty, and then a fist hammered him between the shoulders and he was driven into the waiting fists in the shadows.

Three of them!

And they had him caught in a triangle of pain and jarring blows now, working him as they wanted in the confined space of the lane, jamming him into a corner where two buildings met. Santee did what he could but three was just one too many. Giving his attention one way, there were now two other directions they could come at him.

And they did: one had got in behind him so he could not use the corner to protect his back.

His legs were rubber. All of them, including Santee himself, had trampled on his gunnysack underfoot. One man stumbled and Santee took advantage of it, drove his shoulder against him, opening a way out of the triangle. He had lost his hat and his shirt was ripped and he ached and throbbed. If he could have gotten his gun it would have ended right there with him standing in the midst of three corpses.

But — no gun. Too many experienced roughnecks — and an open stretch of lane leading to the telegraph office and a few small buildings. He chose this way, swayed and zigzagged as he started to run. His legs were weaker than he expected. His boots kicked something — *that damn gunnysack again!* He felt himself falling . . . and heard the trio leaping towards him.

He was now in the worst possible position, lying prone, and the boots started thudding into his lean body even before he could cover his head with his arms.

Then — 'What the hell's goin' on here!'

The kicking stopped and through blurring vision he saw the trio snap their heads around.

The telegraph man had apparently been locking up his office for the night and seen the attack. He had been robbed once himself in that dark lane, and threatened twice more — that was why he now carried a sawn-off shotgun whenever he didn't close till after dark. And a shaft of fugitive light streaked along the dark barrels now as he lifted the weapon, covering the trio standing over the battered man at their feet. He let them hear the hammers snapping back.

'Git! Or I'll use this!'

The trio didn't hesitate. They turned and ran back towards the Square end of the lane. Arch Thomas watched them go, stepped closer to Santee who was staggering upright.

'Better come inside and let's take a look at you.'

Santee nodded, taking the man's offered arm as they moved slowly towards the telegraph office. Suddenly, he pulled back against the telegraph man. 'My gun — it's on the ground somewhere back there.'

'I'll look for it after I get you patched up.'

'You recognize any of 'em?'

'Just one. Ornery bastard named Olly Patch. Used to be a deputy, but Walt had to fire him for bein' too rough with his prisoners. He'd have no trouble pickin' up a coupla sidekicks to help him in somethin' like this.'

Limping, Santee took the man's arm again and allowed himself to be led towards the telegraph office, thinking, *Those two silver dollars are likely going to turn out to be the best couple of bucks I ever spent.*

4

Blessing Or Curse?

The split in his lower lip was going to be annoying — and painful — Santee knew from past experience. It would hurt and swell up during the night, sting like fury when it was touched by the hot rim of a coffee mug, scraped by food like crisp bacon, and split wide open every time he yawned.

'Goddamnit!' he growled, after Arch Thomas had cleaned up some of the grazes and bruises elsewhere on his face. The point of one shoulder showed through a rip in his shirt, the flesh torn by a boot sole. In such an awkward place the telegraph man had been unable to cover it with anything that would stay in place.

'I'll get something when I go back to the hotel, Arch — *gracias*.'

'Forget it. But if you checked out you won't get back into the hotel tonight.' Santee looked at him quizzically. 'Din' you notice all the cowboys in town? Tom Eastman's crew's arrived with his herd. Be no spare rooms tonight, hotel nor whorehouse.'

Santee had noticed a lot of men in range clothes moving about town. 'I'll camp out till sun-up, then ride on.'

Thomas was looking at him speculatively. 'I got a spare bunk at my shack. Ain't no hotel but you'll be safe enough there. I live alone. Wife died years ago.'

Santee frowned. 'Safe enough? Now you've found my Colt, I'm safe enough.'

'Yeah, but that might not've been just a chance attack to roll you for your money in the lane. If it wasn't, someone could make another try for you.'

'Possible,' Santee allowed. But that would mean Bascombe and possibly Waters were truly involved in what had happened to Josh Rankin. He hadn't figured that earlier, just rousted them a little, to see what it might produce. 'Damn, I wish I'd got to Bale before he quit town.'

'Eddie Bale? Prison guard?' Santee nodded and Thomas said, 'He's gone on leave; sent a wire to some gal up in Phoenix tellin' her to expect him in a day or so.'

'Phoenix? Waters thinks he's gone to Nevada or Oregon.'

'No. I got a copy of the wire in my message record book . . . ' Thomas was moving as he spoke in the cramped back room of the telegraph office, went through to the front and came back, leafing through a book with stiff black cardboard covers. 'Here y'are. Bale sent his wire to Miss Dee Brandison, care of Butterfly House.' He lifted his gaze, smiled crookedly. 'That's a whorehouse on Pike Street. He says he'll be there in two days — so he's there by now, I guess.'

'Thanks, Arch, you've been a damn good help.' Santee started to dig into his pocket but Thomas shook his head.

'I don't want no money. The glimpse I got of Olly Patch in the lane, bleeding plenty from his nose an' mouth, is payment enough just to know that son of a bitch got some come-uppance.' He closed the book. 'Telegraph wires can be a blessin', or a curse, can't they? Eddie Bale sends off a message that makes him feel mighty good, somethin' to look forward to. And that same message is gonna kick his legs out from under him when you find him!' His mouth twisted. 'Another one who can stand bein' took down a few pegs: but I guess he's no rougher than the other guards. Not that some of them cons don't deserve it, but Waters don't rein in any of his guards, gives 'em a free-hand, short of killin'.'

'Not so sure about that part, either,' Santee allowed, thinking of how convenient it was that Navajo Joe had fallen off the wall and drowned.

It was almost mid-morning when Santee moved stiffly into the telegraph office and Arch Thomas looked up from writing in a small notebook beside his Morse key.

'Find the grub I left for you?'

Santee nodded, patted his stomach. 'Cooked it and ate the lot — hope that was OK.' Thomas waved a hand. 'I should've told you to wake me earlier.'

'Hell, you took a good lickin' last night. How you feel? *Really* feel, I mean? Like I shoulda woke you at sunup? Or let you snore on a mite longer?'

Santee smiled. 'OK. Thanks, Arch. Any messages for me?'

'Yep — from your friend Scully.' He took a yellow form off a spike and handed it to Santee who read it quickly.

'Hell! That brand on the girl's horse don't seem to be known anywhere.' Santee shook the form. 'If Sandy Scully can't trace it, it's like it don't exist, yet Navajo was clear enough about seeing it.'

'Might not be just a ranch brand,' Thomas pointed out. 'Could belong to a livery or stables that run their own string of mounts.'

'Reckon Sandy would've checked on that.'

'Well, s'pose she come up from Sonora? Nothin' to say she weren't Mexican was there?'

Santee straightened, wincing slightly as subtle pain shot through his ribs. 'You're right! We're close enough to the Border. Joe even said she could be Mexican. Guess I'm still half-asleep, Arch.'

Thomas was sober now. 'Mebbe, but if you hadn't stayed at my place last night, you'd likely be dead.'

'How come?' Santee had gone very still, face sober.

'First, which room did you have at the hotel?'

'Number seven.'

Thomas nodded. 'That's the one. Gent who hired it after you checked out was shot to death through the window by someone with a shotgun in the early hours of the mornin'.'

'The hell you say!'

'That's what happened, Jim. Now you ride careful, *amigo*, you've trod on a lot of toes down here, a heap harder than you know.'

'And I'll do it again.'

He had thought about calling in on Sheriff Walt Bascombe before leaving town to prod him some about the man who had died in Santee's old room. But he changed his mind, rode his mount through the wide livery doors and turned towards the north.

Arch Thomas had sent another wire to Sandy Scully, suggesting the origin of the triangle-double-X brand might be south of the Border. He promised to forward any reply to Jim, care of General Delivery, Gila Bend. Or, if the reply didn't come in for a few days, he would send it on in an attempt to catch up with him at Phoenix.

Marvellous thing, the telegraph, Santee allowed, as he rode away from Yuma, dropping into cover as soon as he could, checking his backtrail. So far it seemed OK, but this was still close to town: he would check again in another hour or so.

Meantime, looking up at the sun streaking along the copper wire strung on the telegraph poles beside the trail, his jaw hardened — and his split lip popped open, bringing a sharp oath from him.

'Yeah. Golden wire, delivering a blessing or a *goddamn curse!*' he gritted, and the horse whinnied a slight protest as he involuntarily tightened his grip on the reins and sawed with the bit. He eased off the pressure. 'Sorry, boy.' He dabbed at the bleeding lip. 'Mind wandered onto somethin' I'd rather forget.'

Not that he ever *could* forget what thinking about the telegraph had stirred within him again. The ugly thoughts had been swirling around in his head ever since young Josh's murder. He had done his best to keep them pushed to the back of his mind, but now, at last, something was beginning to move and he needed to utilize every bit of knowledge he could rake up. Trying to ignore it was no longer profitable or wise. *Josh's murder had happened because of a goddamn telegraph message!*

Definitely no 'blessing' that time: it was a 'curse' of the worst kind, and it would stay with him for the rest of his life.

* * *

During his travels with Josh throughout Arizona, searching for and buying good breeding stock for the senator's ranching project, Santee had checked in every town that had a telegraph. It was important that he stayed in touch with the governor's office.

In a place called Casa Grande, where they were to be met by representatives of a rancher named Heath Dakin, who ran a huge spread with top breeding cows and seed bulls, Santee walked to the telegraph station while Josh, more than a little the worse for drink from the night before, soaked in a hot tub, moaning that never again would he so much as sniff the cork of a whiskey bottle. Not that he was a heavy drinker: in fact, that was the problem — Josh wasn't used to a lot of liquor, but he was desperate to be accepted as 'one of the boys' by these hard-drinking, hard-playing roughnecks he admired so much. Dared and light-heartedly bullied, he had gone into town to the saloon and allowed Dakin's ranch hands to show him one last high time as a bachelor before he was 'manacled' by marriage, as one of them put it.

Apparently, it had quickly gotten out of hand and Josh was paying for his excesses this particular morning. Santee had never seen him so down and it was mighty unusual for him to be so surly. He seemed slow and stiff in his movements, snapped Jim's head off when he asked if he'd been in a brawl.

'What I've *been in* is no concern of yours, Santee! You're hired help and I don't have to tell you a damn thing!

And I sure as hell don't need your *help*!'

Santee read that as meaning he did need his help, a back-to-front plea. Josh was essentially a good type and such a wild night must've hurt him, likely stricken his conscience . . . 'specially if there had been an episode with a whore arranged in his 'interests' by the roughneck cowboys. Josh was devoted to Deborah Burdin and would quickly settle into marriage and never stray from the matrimonial path in Santee's opinion. He and Deborah had a fine future ahead of them. The senator was taking a chance on Josh's talents, but so far it seemed like the gamble was paying off: Josh was astute in selecting the animals he wanted, demanded proof of all claims made, and persuasive when it came to dickering over the price. He was good-natured under all circumstances even when these hard-living cowhands played some pretty boisterous jokes on him. *But not this time!*

Sometimes he got his own back, and this only lifted their respect for the young Californian: he had a good wide streak of devilment in him and enjoyed the challenge of exacting his own form of revenge.

Except he wouldn't talk about it this time: usually, self-consciously, he would tell Santee how he had been suckered into some kind of prank, but he was in too black a mood to even discuss it now. So Santee had left it, walked to the telegraph station, figuring Josh would come round in his own good time, once his hangover had cleared up.

There were two messages waiting for him. One was from Senator Rankin requesting an honest report on his son's performance, whether, in Santee's opinion, Josh was really cut out for a ranching kind of life, at managerial level, or was he finding the deals too difficult to handle yet was still trying hard in order to please his father?

'He's got a lot of brains, Senator,'

Santee said to himself, mentally composing his positive reply. 'And he can sweet-talk these so-called hard-nosed ranchers into selling at *his* price. He'll run a good spread and at a profit.'

But, before Santee could send off that message, the second wire stopped him in his tracks: it was from Deborah.

PLEASE MEET ME STAGE SWING-STATION AT MEMORY CREEK. URGENT. DO NOT TELL JOSH. I HAVE TERRIBLE NEWS AND MUST TELL HIM IN PERSON. COME QUICKLY. DEB-DEB.

It was the 'Deb-Deb' that convinced Santee the message was genuine. When she had first known him after the battle with the stage robbers, her obvious crush on him and naïve admiration had sent him into many a fluster: she would suddenly appear beside him and amuse herself by forcing him to back away when she deliberately came too close, saying mischievous and intentionally embarrassing things. She gave him little time to protest, so that often he stammered over her name: 'Deb-Deb — *Deborah*! Now you quit this foolishness, right now, dammit!'

Later, when she came to her senses, they found they could both laugh at those times in retrospect. But it was strictly between the two of them: she would never embarrass him in company with such outrageous behaviour these days. So, when he saw the DEB-DEB on the message form his stomach knotted.

Here was real trouble. He had no idea what it could be, but if Deborah was coming in person it must be mighty important.

Josh Rankin, recovered from his depression or not, would have to handle his last — and biggest — deal with Dakin alone, now. It couldn't be helped: Santee was confident he would manage, anyway. *He* had no option but to meet Deborah and pronto.

So he made his excuses — couldn't even remember what they were now

— had suggested some ideas to help get the transaction started, and then he had ridden fast to his rendezvous with the girl.

Except she wasn't there: the swing-station itself wasn't there — only its charred remains. It had burned down six months earlier and now only a few blackened boards were still standing, creaking and swaying in the hot wind.

There wasn't much left, but sufficient to hide the rifleman who shot Santee's horse out from under him.

As he catapulted over the falling animal's head Santee snatched his own rifle from the saddle scabbard, and threw himself to one side. He hit rolling and kept going, sensing rather than hearing or seeing the spurts of dirt as a volley of slugs sought him.

He rolled in against the back of the dying mount, pretty sure the ambusher had emptied his magazine in that volley — damn fool! Now, while he reloaded, Santee's eagle-sharp eyes saw movement through a warped gap in the charred timber, which didn't look very thick. He leaned on the shuddering horse, pumped out four fast shots, saw the black dust and splinters showering. He heard the startled grunt of the killer, watched through the gap as the man sprawled, then stumbled trying to get to his feet. Santee leapt over the now dead horse, ran forward. He glimpsed the white face of the beard-shagged man who fell half on his back as he brought his partly loaded rifle up, shooting wild.

Santee kicked aside the charred planks and leapt at the killer now struggling to his feet, wet redness showing on one side of his sweaty shirt. He had dropped his rifle and snatched at his six-gun. Santee dived right, rolling, landing on his shoulder and spinning around, firing his rifle one-handed.

The man's six-gun blasted, but jumped from his hand, and the ambusher gagged and spread out on his face. Santee used a boot toe under his shoulder to roll him onto his back. He was a stranger, had the look of some saloon hanger-on who could be hired for a dirty dollar. Santee placed his boot over the bleeding wound and the man began to writhe, screaming and thrashing frantically in pain.

'Who hired you?'

Panting, as Santee eased up a little, the man spat and tried to pick up his six-gun. He slapped the barrel across Santee's shins. Jim staggered, his hand closing convulsively on the rifle's trigger.

The muzzle was only six inches away, and directly above the centre of the dry-guicher's chest —

★   ★   ★

Forking the dead man's horse — unbranded and with no information in the saddlebags — Santee rode to the nearest town. No one had seen Deborah, knew of her or had even heard of her, for that matter, anywhere in the district.

There was no time to wire Prescott to check if she was still there: he had to get back to Josh. Someone had successfully separated them and Santee's hunch told him the reason for it was all too apparent.

His sense of disaster tore at him as he rode the horse savagely, like when training for a war-party with half-tame mustangs, back in his days with the Sioux.

But he was too late: Josh was already dead.

He rode back to the fire-gutted swing-station and brought in the body of the man who had bushwhacked him. No one knew him: he was not a local hardcase. The telegraphs began to sing that night — and daytime, too — messages humming between Casa Grande and Prescott — and California.

No one needed to tell him that Josh's murderers had to be found, that the youth had to be avenged.

No matter how long it took. Or who fell to Santee's gun in the process.

He could never face Deborah or the governor or Senator Rankin until he had found Josh's killer.

Now, with Yuma at last dropping from sight behind him, Jim Santee felt that he was once again on the right trail, and he was quite willing to make himself a target if it would flush the killers out.

Then he would watch them all die — through the gunsmoke from his Colt or rifle.

5

Tall Target

Sitting his mount on a shaded ledge now, Santee rolled and lit a cigarette, leaning on the saddlehorn as he smoked and surveyed the country surrounding him.

So far, his backtrail was clear and he could not tell for sure that the trail ahead was safe, but his hunch was that it, too, was clear — for now.

The sun was hot and he loosened his shirt collar, feeling a wash of cooler air on his throat. He lifted his hat and scratched at his sweat-soaked dark hair. *It didn't seem quite right* — that was his gut-feeling. He had been jumped in the alley and things had been getting pretty damn vicious when Arch Thomas had come to his rescue. Then, whoever had set up the attack had, quite logically, assumed he would go back to his hotel room — maybe they didn't know he had already quit it. But someone else had unsuspectingly hired the room and was now resting forever in a hole in the sun-hardened ground of Yuma's Boot Hill.

By now, they must know he was still alive and it wouldn't need a genius to check the trails out of town to see which way he was headed. Then why didn't someone follow? Or was someone already in position ahead, waiting for him to ride into a headshot taken from the cover of a boulder or a broken ridge?

That was more likely! Because he — or anyone — had to ride as far as this point before they could pick up the main trails — north, east, west.

He straightened slightly to flick away the cigarette butt and, as he did so, he glanced at the distorted sawtoothed shadow of the rocks that shaded his ledge, towering behind where he sat and something moved along the small section that was visible to him.

A crouching man who held a rifle, and — *two of them!*

Well, he was the foolish one: he had chosen this place as the only one high enough to give him a good view over the country he aimed to travel through and whoever was waiting for him knew damn well this was where he would have to come in order to check out the land.

So they had been settled in, maybe even long before he had left town and he had blindly obliged them by following their logic. Now, they were ready to make their move.

The high ridge gave them the advantage. He was out on the ledge and it was narrow enough to need some reining back and forth in order to turn his mount so as to head down to the sandy slope below, which, in turn, led into the snaking dry wash below that.

He would make a fine target, manoeuvring his horse virtually on the one spot; they could even take their time to draw bead, pick him off when they were good and ready.

The only other way out — if it was a way out — was to leap the horse off the ledge and let it drop onto the sloping sand below the ledge, hoping it wouldn't break a leg or its neck — or *his* neck! *Damned dangerous*, but . . .

By now, the men above were in position, would already be lining him up in their sights.

No more time to waste! He wrenched the startled mount's head around, jammed home the spurs and flicked the reins, letting out a wild war whoop.

Long, hard muscles bunched under him. A shrill whinny assailed his ears — and then he rocked in leather as the horse launched itself off the ledge.

At the same time, two guns blazed from above. He heard a snarl as one bullet passed his face on the left side, a whining ricochet as the second one struck the ledge and sprayed stone chips.

Then the world fell away beneath him.

And, seconds later, jarred him so hard he thought the base of his spine was broken. He half-spilled from the saddle. Bullets whipped past his rocking body as he instinctively fought the reins and strived for control of his own body, using his weight to the best advantage. The horse shrilled and rocked, started to go down, as he threw his weight towards the rump. The animal buckled its rear legs, propped the forelegs. Sand spewed and fanned out. He felt the horse going over and kicked his boots free of the stirrups, hurled himself awkwardly to the side, snatching at his rifle in the scabbard.

His hand slipped off the smooth wood of the stock and then he was spinning on to his back, feeling the sandy gravel sliding away beneath him. He held his Colt in leather as gravity took over. Sliding, virtually out of control, he had to dodge the tumbling horse, a hoof slicing past his head, bare inches away. Then, somehow, he was on his belly and the Colt was in his hand as he jerked to a stop.

The gun bucked against his wrist and a man on the rocks above the ledge, rising to get a better shot, twisted away as if kicked by a mule. The second man, beside him, had his rifle half-raised, the lever closing as he jacked another shell into the breech. Shocked, he paused to stare at his companion. *Bad mistake*.

Santee's next shot clipped the rock and ricocheted slicing across the killer's chest. He flipped backwards out of sight.

Santee crouched, glanced at his horse as it struggled up, looking dazed, limping, but mostly unhurt. He began to crab his way across.

Then a harsh voice said, 'By Godfrey, you are straight outa hell, ain't you, Santee!' A bullet kicked gravel into his face.

He spun, slipping, glimpsed a man he recognized from the brawl in the alley. *Olly Patch*. And he was holding a smoking rifle sighted on his body.

'Uh-uh! Don't try to use that Colt again, Santee! I'd rather have you alive, but you wanna push it' — he shrugged heavy shoulders — 'you choose!'

Santee, only half-balanced, swayed erect and lifted his hands shoulder high. A jerk of the rifle barrel told him to lose the six-gun. Reluctantly, he let it fall at his feet.

Patch called loudly, voice echoing from the rocks, 'You boys OK?'

A shaky voice answered from the rocks. 'Like hell! I been sliced by a ricochet — bleedin' plenty . . .'

'That's you, Blackie,' Patch called, without a trace of sympathy or concern. 'What about Spangler?'

'He don't look so good, Olly,' Blackie answered. 'Think he's goin' fast.'

'The hell . . . I am!' sobbed a sick-sounding voice. 'I ain't goin' . . . till I square with that son of a *bitch*! He's busted my shoulder!'

Olly Patch laughed. 'Runnin' true to form, Spang! Bitch, bitch, bitch. Well, crawl on down here. We got us some talkin' to do to this 'breed — *my* kinda talkin'!'

Patch leered at Santee and the two wounded men staggered down, helping each other. They made a sorry pair, hard, rough men who would kick their own mother down a flight of stairs for a dollar-and-a-half. Mixed with the pain in their eyes was a savage desire for vengeance on the man who had wounded them.

Santee watched, face expressionless, hands still raised.

Spangler, the one with the shattered shoulder, moaned and swore bitterly as Blackie the one with the ricochet gash across his chest, made a rough sling from two bandannas tied together and wadded a grubby rag over the bleeding wound.

Panting, Spangler collapsed onto a rock and Patch tossed Blackie his own neckerchief. He caught it, held it to the short gash across his upper chest, the shock wearing off now as he glared at Santee.

'Gimme first crack at him, Ol!' Blackie gasped. 'I had him lined up but he was too damn fast!'

'He's mine!' grated Spangler, but it was obvious that though his hate might be driving him, he had little energy to spare and almost fell as he tried to stand up.

Patch chuckled. 'See, 'breed? You is popular!'

'Wh-why don't we kill him, Ol?'

'All in good time, Blackie. Hey, Santee, help us out, OK? How much d'you know?'

'Not enough.'

Patch laughed. 'Well, you gonna have to spell that one out, or you'll find yourself missin' a coupla body parts you might have some use for some-time!'

'I'll do that bit!' Blackie volunteered, reaching for his hunting knife on his belt. But it had slipped around to the back and he swore, gave up, gasping: his chest felt as if it were being crushed, torn muscles cramped by his arm movement. He glared at Santee. 'I'll get to you yet!'

Olly Patch moved to a rock, still holding his rifle on Santee, motioned that he could lower his arms. 'Just don't move. You gonna tell us what you know, or do I give Blackie a hand to get his knife?'

'What I know you can stuff in a flea's ear. All I know for sure is Josh Rankin's dead. Murdered by some pale-haired son of a bitch, who also beat up and raped a young woman who happened upon 'em, helped by a bunch of trail scum. They dumped her in the river.'

Patch was sober now. 'And . . . ?'

'Senator Rankin sent me to find out who killed Josh, but don't make the mistake of thinking he's after justice: he wants revenge.'

Patch's face straightened and for an instant a cloud passed behind his eyes. Then he curled a lip.

'An' you're the avenger, huh?' Santee said nothing. 'Well, well, well, them old boys stick together, don't they? Governor and senator upholdin' the law an' all that hogwash! *As long as it suits 'em!*' He spat, mouth in an ugly twist now. 'But when it gits personal, they'll bend it like a goddamned pretzel! Hypocritical bastards!'

Santee waited silently, knowing Olly was expecting an answer.

'O-K! Well, you dunno much, do you, 'breed? We got nothin' to worry about, boys.' Olly glanced at his wounded pards, smiling crookedly. 'This sonuver don't even know who he's chasin'.'

'You could tell me.'

Olly's short laugh was more like an explosion of scorn. 'I could tell you lots of things, but I ain't gonna. What I'm gonna do is leave you to Blackie and Spangler: reckon they'll find some way of amusin' themselves for a while before they finish you off.'

'Hey! That's good, huh, Spang?'

Spangler's shattered shoulder was giving him hell. His eyelids drooped, but there was plenty of hatred evident in them. 'Ye-ah.' He turned his pain-filled gaze to Olly Patch. 'Where you goin'?'

'Where I was told to: Phoenix.'

'Phoenix!' Blackie's mouth hung open in surprise. 'Judas priest, why the hell Phoenix?'

'That's where Bale went. He ain't visitin' no kin in Nevada or Oregon like he said, he's got hisself a leetle ol' whore stashed away in Phoenix.'

'Well, smoke me!'

'You — you better help me get to a sawbones first, Ol,' Spangler grated, somewhat pathetically. 'I dunno as I can handle this much longer. I feel bone . . . gratin'.'

'Blackie can get you to a doc's. I've wasted enough time. Boss said to stop Santee an' we've done that. You two can make it permanent. *Come on*! Get your guns on him! Or you want me to save you the trouble?'

'No! No trouble, for Chris'sakes!' snapped Blackie, his gun in hand now, his shirt front soaked with blood, but it was obvious the wound was not all that serious. 'It'll be a whole heap of *fun*, won't it, Spang?'

Spangler nodded dully, trying to make his hatred work for him, drive his adrenalin past the pain in his crippled shoulder. He even managed to slip his Colt out of the holster and clumsily cocked the hammer — his thumb was slippery with his own blood. The barrel wavered in Santee's general direction 'I-I just might not be able to . . . hit you where I'm . . . aimin', 'breed.' He started to chuckle but it changed to a cough. 'So — so you can 'xpect . . . 'xpect a lotta pain — dependin' where my lead lands!'

Blackie grinned. 'That sounds like a good idea, Spang! We'll practise our shootin' with Mr 'Breed Santee as the target!'

Olly Patch nodded. 'You boys seem to have the right idea. Just don't take too long. He's a tricky bastard.'

As he turned away, Santee said, 'Who is this killer with the white hair, Patch?'

Olly looked over his shoulder. 'Think I'm gonna tell you?'

'Well, don't seem like I'm gonna be able to pass it along to anyone — 'cept the Devil.'

Olly smiled crookedly. 'Ain't that a fact? But you're just gonna have to die not knowin', 'breed, but I'll say this: even if you did know, you'll never be able to touch him . . . *adios!*'

As he moved off, Blackie called, 'We go back to the spread when we're through here, Ol?'

'Yeah, get yourselves patched up in town first. Tell the boss I'll be back after I fix Bale.'

He had a horse behind the rocks and Santee heard the saddle leather creak as the man mounted. Then he appeared, forking a big grey, glanced once towards the trio and rode off towards the tangle of canyons and dry washes ahead and below.

Blackie kept watch on him until he was out of sight. Spangler was being more and more affected by his wound:

his collarbone was broken and Santee knew the man must be nearly out of his head with the extreme pain. He was pretty tough to be standing up to things as well as he was. Santee shuffled his feet, looking down.

His Colt still lay on the ground not a yard from his boots.

Close, but so damn far, too. It might seem easy, throw himself at the gun, scoop it up and blast the men who were going to kill him a little at a time. But all the movements involved took time — milliseconds, maybe, but these men were burning with hatred for him and already had their guns in their hands, eager to start his torment.

Still, *what did he have to lose?* He was going to die anyway, whether it was now or a couple of hours later when death would come as a relief from the agony he would be suffering made little difference.

A Santee Sioux never died without a fight. Never!

Blackie surprised him. He whirled

suddenly, staggered a little, but quickly found his footing and fired. He aimed low — at Santee's crotch. But his own wound had taken more toll than he figured and his aim was off.

The bullet seared across Santee's left hip, spinning him off balance. He was falling away from his Colt but twisted back so he would fall on or near the gun.

Despite his pain-dulled brain, Spangler had enough sense to see what was happening, brought up his gun and fired. It was wild as he swayed, and Blackie yelled, ducking as the bullet whipped air close to him.

'*Christ almighty!* The hell're you doin'?'

He straightened, attention on Spangler who was trying desperately to raise his Colt.

Too late.

Santee's hand closed around the butt of his six-gun and he spun on to his side, bringing it into the open, triggering. Boom-boom! A double crash that sounded like one prolonged shot.

Blackie was thrown back a yard as the bullets slammed into him, just below his throat. He went down choking on his own blood.

Boom! Santee's Colt blasted again: his last shot, and it took Spangler just above the belt buckle. The man writhed, screaming and choking.

Santee was already on his feet, shucking out the used shells from the cylinder, replacing them with fresh loads from his belt. Holding the gun, hammer spur under his thumb, he walked across to stand above Spangler who was twisting in agony, eyes bulging and staring, hands clawing into the dirt, blood bubbling through the hand pressed into the midriff wound, holding back part of an intestine.

'Help . . . me!'

'You want a quick death, Spangler? Or one like you had planned for me?'

Spangler coughed blood and Santee hunkered down beside him.

'You must've been a bad boy. You're

gonna have a terrible death — unless you tell me a few things I need to know. You got time: I'll see to that. Know just how to keep you with me long enough till I find out what I want.'

'You lousy damn . . . *Injun!* I-I'm sufferin'!'

Santee grinned coldly.

'Yeah, well, I'm feelin' more Injun than white man today, Spangler,' Santee said casually enough. 'That makes you one unlucky son of a bitch.'

6

Butterflies

The livery man in the stables that fronted the plaza looked at the scarred flanks on the sweaty dun horse. He was a big man wearing a grimy scuffed leather apron and he glared at Santee as the man off-saddled.

'You'd do this hoss a big favour if you modified your spur rowels, mister.' His voice was cold with barely controlled anger.

Santee glanced at the man over his shoulder, then lifted his left leg, bending it at the knee. The stable man frowned when he saw the rowel was made from a silver dollar, without any serrations or spikes.

'They never carved up this poor hoss like them scars show!'

'Made from my first winnings in a

poker game where no one tried to cheat me.' Santee held the man's puzzled stare. 'You look like a 'breed, you're fair game.'

'Well, ain't you? A 'breed, I mean.'

'No. Now that's all the explanation you get — except this ain't my hoss. I borrowed it from a feller had no more use for it. Mine made a jump off a ledge, twisted its foreleg some, so I turned it loose not far from town. It'll rest up for a day or so, then go looking for someone to care for it.'

The big man scratched at his balding head, ran a tongue briefly across his lips, seeing the dangerous look this ranny had — and he hadn't noticed earlier because he was so mad at finding a mistreated horse.

'Guess I spoke outa turn.'

'Forget it. Where's Pike Street?'

The livery man smiled crookedly. 'That street sure is popular! Like a dollar for every ranny hits town and asks the way.'

'If it'll get me an answer . . . ' Santee

said, thumbing a dollar out of his pocket and offering it to the man.

'Aw — no, no. I was just joshin'. You turn right outa my main doors, cross the plaza, walk the block till you come to the druggist's on the corner and that's Pike Street.'

'Obliged. Butterfly House far along?'

'The Butterfly! Man, I hope you're well heeled.'

Wearily, Santee proffered the dollar again. 'You chasin' this again?'

A big calloused hand lifted. 'Sorry. It's about middle of the street, north side. You'll see the sign.' The words faded slowly as he saw Santee slide his rifle out of the saddle scabbard. 'You ain't gonna carry that through town though. Reason I say, we got us a ding-dong marshal here, Kelly Sanchez, and his deputies are just as keen as he is.'

Santee unbuckled the scabbard from his saddle while the hostler was speaking, slid the rifle into leather. 'How about like this?'

'Some better, but they're likely to give you a hard time.'

Santee merely nodded. 'Give the hoss what he needs.'

'He can do with a damn good curry-combin' for a start . . . an' lookit them ribs! You say the feller owned him don't want him no more?'

'I said he didn't have any more use for him: he's dead.'

The livery man stared a long minute, then nodded slowly. 'I hope he didn't die too fast.'

Santee said nothing, shouldered the rifle and walked out through the doors. He swung across the plaza through the traffic of wagons and buckboards and buggies, a tall, rawboned man, dark Indian features causing more than one rider dodging his horse around him to swallow the curse that rose to his lips.

Jim Santee was mighty weary. It had been a long, hard ride. The dun had belonged to Spangler. He had ridden Blackie's sorrel before that but it, too, had been neglected and out of consideration for the suppurating sore on the fetlock, he had unsaddled it and turned it loose in a small sandy canyon with grass and a water-hole.

He felt no remorse about the dead men he had left back there in the draw at the foot of the high ledge. The world would not miss their kind.

Catching up with Olly Patch had been unsuccessful, though. For one thing, the dun had been ridden hard and neglected for too long, was unable to make the effort Santee required. He tried to urge it along twice, but saw it was only going to be temporary at best, and each time exhausted the horse even more.

So, with Indian-learned patience, he had allowed it to more or less make its own pace. Now, he hoped he wasn't too late.

*   *   *

The Butterfly House was unmistakable — there was a huge wooden cut-out of a butterfly in flight painted yellow and black, with two large red eyes. It was fixed to the adobe wall above an arched entrance that led into a flagged courtyard with hitching facilities and a series of stalls for the mounts of men who figured on staying longer than just an hour or so — and had the money to pay for it.

A short, hard-faced man dressed like a Mexican *caballero* appeared and greeted him in Spanish, his jaw hardening when he saw the rifle. He gestured to a narrow entrance with a red-painted door.

'Check your guns in there, *señor*.'

'S'pose I don't want to check 'em?'

The man shrugged, gaze steady and cool. 'I whistle, and you go straight back through the gateway.'

Testing, Santee said, 'Maybe.'

The man shook his head once, gestured with a finger, pointing to a small balcony above the red door. A man sat there in a straightback chair. He was cradling a shotgun, looked to be dozing, but Santee wouldn't bet on it.

He nodded curtly. 'Guess I'm lucky to be getting as far as the red door.'

'*Sí, señor*,' the man said with heavy emphasis. 'You have been told the rules.'

'And I savvy them, *amigo*. You got a gal here called Dee Brandison?'

'Brandy? Oh, yes.' He ran his gaze up and down Santee's worn and dusty trail clothes. 'She come expensive.'

'Uh-huh. I'll manage. Friend of mine asked me to meet him here — name of Bale?'

Was that a flicker in the dark eyes? The hard face didn't change. 'Bale, *señor*?'

'Your hearing's all right.'

'He is popular, this Señor Bale. You are the second man to ask for him today.'

Santee tensed slightly, moving his feet so as to cover it. 'That so?'

The *caballero* nodded. 'A man a little bigger than you, heavier, though not

111

quite as tall. He smell of many trails and have a face that had met someone else's fists not too long ago.' The man's dark gaze dropped to Santee's hands with their skinned and bruised knuckles. There was a slight query on the hard face when he looked squarely at Jim again.

'Sounds like someone I might know. When was he here?'

'He still upstairs. He had spent the night in another house, across the street. It is called Ladybird — the owner liked our name but could not use it so he pick another insect. I think your frien' say he had made a mistake, had meant to come here in the first place.'

'But he stayed the night over there?'

A shrug. 'Is cheaper — and they say the ladies are more adventurous. Not many men visit short-time only.'

And Olly Patch wasn't the type who would deny himself a chance at some exotic bedroom adventures . . .

The gun-check counter was just inside the door and there were two men

112

with crossed gunbelts and twin holsters standing one at either end. A third man behind the counter, piled with tagged guns of all description, stood behind it. He held a yellow square of paper in his hand.

'Dollar an hour to park your weapons, friend,' he said with a leering smile. 'Not *all* your weapons, of course, but them you won't be needin' upstairs. Gets cheaper the longer you stay.'

Santee slapped a dollar on the counter and as the man wrote on the yellow chit, unbuckled his gunbelt and laid the rifle on the counter with the six-gun rig. The man was tying small numbered white tags on to the trigger guards when the two gun-hung men came up on either side of Santee.

'You don't mind a quick search, do you — sir?'

Rough hands were working over his body in an expert way before Santee could answer. They took his knife, put it with his guns.

'A necessary ritual, friend.'

Santee was about to move away when there was a gunshot from upstairs and a scream, followed by a door slamming and more gunshots.

'Looks like you missed one!' Santee said, sprinting for the stairs. The nearest man reached for him and Santee swung back, butted him in the face with the top of his head and whipped a revolver from one of the man's fancy holsters. The second guard was skidding to a stop, dragging one of his pistols free. He froze when Santee waved the cocked gun in his face.

'Whoa! Listen, stay outa the way, mister! This is our business,' the guard growled.

'I've a hunch it's mine!'

Santee gun-whipped the man to his knees beside his dazed, bloody-faced companion, turned and sprinted up the stairs.

The screaming had not stopped and was ringing loud in his ears as he reached the landing. He dropped flat as he glimpsed Olly Patch crouched beside a door and a struggling, wild-eyed, half-naked woman pinned to the floor by one of his knees.

Olly's face was a study in shock as he recognized Santee and then he yanked the girl to her feet and pulled her in front of him, shooting at Santee. He backed into a room with a door hanging by one hinge.

She screamed again and Olly cuffed her briefly with the gun barrel, bringing a sob from her as he moved into the room, shooting again. Santee rolled across the landing, snapped a shot. Splinters flew from the doorframe. Patch was dragging the sagging girl towards a window now, balcony rails visible beyond.

A man lay sprawled on his face across a bed with black and red silk sheets. Santee had the impression it was Eddie Bale — though he had never seen the man in his underwear before, only his prison guard's uniform. He wasn't moving and the red on the black sheet under him looked more like blood than crimson silk.

Patch held the girl awkwardly, one arm under hers, around her waist, also gripping his smoking gun. With his free hand he hurled a chair through the window. Glass shattered and flimsy wood framing splintered.

The girl was hindering him now, He had hit her too hard and she was only half-conscious, her sagging weight making him stumble. With a roaring oath he flung her across the room towards Santee, fired again and started to climb out of the window.

Santee dived for the floor, skidded across the highly polished timber and a furry rug, dodging the crumpled girl. Olly swung back, almost out of the window now, threw down with his Colt and triggered.

The hammer fell on an empty chamber.

His eyes widened as he looked down at Santee, whose gun barrel was pointing at him unwaveringly. He started to let his pistol fall, giving up, smirking a little.

Santee fired.

★ ★ ★

'He was dead before he hit the street — and some folk down there heard his neck snap: said it sounded like a pistol shot.'

Kelly Sanchez, Marshal of Phoenix, was part Mexican, in his thirties, and his swarthy skin now lent an extra impact to his curt demeanour. He was a deadly serious man — Santee figured he hardly ever smiled: once a day, maybe, when he shaved, just for the hell of it. His two deputies standing by in the furniture-polish smelling office were just as deadpan, neatly dressed, one holding a pistol on Jim Santee.

'Your bullet knocked him clear through the balcony rail,' Sanchez continued, dark eyes unwavering on Santee. 'His gun was empty.'

'Or maybe I wouldn't be standing here now.'

'Someone out in the passage said you had time to see Patch's gun was empty, but you fired anyway.'

'Too late to do anything else.'

'Or too late to want to do anything else.'

Santee sighed. 'He was a murderer, helped torture and violate an innocent girl who walked in on him and some pards after they'd killed a man — I'm referring to Josh Rankin.'

The thin dark eyebrows arched. 'The Californian senator's son? I wish that'd been in my bailiwick. I'd've had his killers long since.'

'Keep dreaming, Sanchez. It's a closed door. They're all guilty, got too much to lose. None of them'll talk. They're damn scared of someone.'

Sanchez eased back in his chair, studying this tough-looking ranny. 'You work for Governor Burdin, you say, but you still don't come into my town like some damn gunfighter and shoot-up its citizens.'

'Olly Patch wasn't a citizen. He came

here to do one thing: kill Eddie Bale — and he did it.'

Sanchez didn't like the implied accusation.

'He should've been checked properly by the Butterfly guards, and I will look into that, Santee.' He nodded to the deputy holding the gun. 'Take him down to the livery for his horse and escort him out of town.'

'Hold it!' Santee stepped back, facing the armed deputies. 'Sanchez, I'm here to ask some questions. You can't answer them, but I think Dee Brandison might.'

'You'll never know.'

Santee sighed. 'Don't be so hard-nosed. A wire to the governor and you'll be out of office, no pension, no respect from the citizens once they take that badge off you. You'll be just another Mex 'breed.' He smiled faintly as Sanchez started to rise, face suffusing with anger. 'I've had lots of experience of the way folk treat 'breeds — or anyone they figure is one, whether or no.'

Sanchez frowned. 'You're part Indian, aren't you?'

Santee shook his head, gave his brief explanation about the Sioux. 'That's not important; your co-operation is. Senator Rankin is the governor's particular friend and he wants Josh Rankin's murder cleared up pronto. He asks that everyone co-operate with me but, if not, he'll bend a lot of rules and make up a few new ones if he has to.'

'I don't like threats, Santee.'

'Me neither — givin' or takin'. But I need to see that gal they call Brandy.'

Sanchez thought about it. Santee watched the struggle, the man's ego forcing him to resist as long as he could hold out, but in the end there was only one thing he could do. 'They tell me she has concussion.'

'Yeah — Olly gun-whipped her, and not gently. She at the sawbone's?'

Sanchez hesitated one more time, unhappy helping this dangerous-looking man. *And in his own law office! That hurt!* 'They're taking care of her at the

Butterfly; I'll give you one hour.'

'Should be enough.'

'It *will* be! You understand, Santee, one hour, that's all! Carey, she's your sister — you go with him. And take your watch!'

Santee snapped his head up as he started for the door, the youngest of the deputies following, fumbling a silver watch from the pocket of his vest.

They crossed the plaza again but when they reached the drugstore on the corner of Pike, Carey said, 'Keep goin', Brandy's room's at the rear of the Butterfly.'

As they kept moving down the block and turned into the next street, Santee said quietly, 'Sister, eh? I'll bet Sanchez loves having you on his staff.'

Carey, young, trying to look tougher than he really was, Santee figured, said with a surly tone, 'I was elected: he had no choice.'

He indicated they should take a lane off to the right and gestured to a long high fence with a gate in it. Santee could see the upper floor of the Butterfly House rising above it. The deputy stopped suddenly and Santee tensed as he turned and saw the man had his hand on his gun butt.

'You go easy on her.'

'I only want to ask her a few questions, kid.'

'You go easy! I'm glad you killed that son of a bitch, Patch. I'd've done it myself when I seen the welt he left on her. She's gonna have a scar.'

Santee scratched at his stubble. 'Well, she's not exactly dependin' on her face, is she?'

'You shut your mouth, you damn 'breed! By God, I dunno as I'll let you see her!'

'Relax, kid. I can shade you easy, you want to push it that far, but it'd be stupid. I just want to know about Eddie Bale and what he might've told her.'

'Eddie?' Carey frowned and let his hand slowly drop away from his gun butt. 'She kinda liked him, I guess. He called her his gal, but she weren't

— you know . . . '

'Hard to have favourites in that game, I guess.'

The deputy nodded. 'Yeah. She's soft-hearted, Brandy, like Ma used to be. Invite any drifter in for a bowl of chilli or hot stew in the winter. Lots of Brandy's customers spill their guts to her an' sometimes she's even able to give 'em good advice.' There was unmistakable pride in his voice and then, suddenly, he said, 'I knew Josh Rankin.'

That got Santee's attention in a hurry. 'Well?'

'Aw, not very — he was a kinda greenhorn, you know? Looked like one, anyways. Didn't seem to *know* a helluva lot. Made him an easy target for a lot o' rough jokes and pranks.'

'Yeah, he had some citified ways — sheltered upbringing. The senator figured some responsibility'd do him good, was gonna help him set up a cattle business.' Santee frowned slightly. 'Kid was desperate to learn how to fit in. Put up with a lot o' raggin' from some of these frontier boys.' He added quietly, 'I think it was what got him killed.'

Carey nodded vigorously. 'They can sure play rough. You don't take it the right way you're finished.' Santee could tell the young deputy was speaking from some experience here. 'Mostly Josh took it in good part, but I had the feelin' that underneath, he wasn't gonna forget someone made a fool of him; that someday, some way, he'd square things.'

'That was Josh. Good-natured, but only up to a point. He liked everything squared away in the end.'

They were standing near the gate in the fence now and Carey made no move to open it. 'They fixed him up with a session with a coupla whores at the Butterfly, but Brandy wouldn't let them get him into any real fixes. Because I'm her brother, he sort of talked to me more'n the others. He told me them cowboys really got him in a fix with their pranks. Started with a rattlesnake in his bed, then a burr under his saddle and a loose cinchstrap — usual stuff. They ain't too brainy. But they went further: they knew of this feller who — well, he liked *fellers* better'n women. You know what I mean? And Josh was a good-lookin' boy. Skin like a gal's and that long hair . . . '

Santee nodded slowly, mouth grim. 'So that's what happened.' At Carey's puzzled look, he hesitated, then said, 'He was usually a bit quiet after he'd fallen for some prank, but he perked up when he managed to get his own back. But not this last time: he was way down there in his boots. Nothing could shake him or cheer him up. Him and me got along OK, usually, but more than once he snarled at me like a damn wolf. Wouldn't talk about it. Not a word. I couldn't get through to him at all. This time it was a helluva lot more serious than usual. And the way he moved — I figured he'd been beaten, too, but not on the face. He damn well wouldn't *talk*!'

'He told me some of it — turned out to be more than a joke. You don't need the details, I guess. He said he felt like trash and was gonna kill those idiots who fixed it up, no matter what. And one man in particular — you can guess who that was.'

Santee nodded: he knew how shaken Josh had been by his encounter. He had refused to continue with the search for good breeding stock: he was obsessed with finding some way to get his own back, something that would satisfy him.

And he was determined to do it without Jim Santee's help . . . the damn little fool!

Santee didn't even know what had happened at that time, didn't even suspect the truth: if he had, things might have been different — way different.

'He gave me the slip: probably went after this feller. At the same time, someone sent me a fake telegraph message that took me away. When I got back, Josh was already dead.'

Carey nodded, seeing the bleakness and bitterness of blame clearly in Santee. 'I dunno what happened, but I think he might've told Brandy something.' His young face hardened. 'That's why I want you to go easy on her. She's been mighty upset since he saw her.'

'I'll go easy as I can, Carey. but I need to find out what she knows if it'll help me catch up with Josh's killers.'

'What happens when you do?'

'The senator gave me enough money to pay for six funerals; I can send for as much more as I need.'

7

Brandy

One side of her face was swollen, bruised, traversed by a short gash — from Patch's Colt's foresight, most likely — that showed seven stitches. The eye on that side was far back in a swollen, discoloured area.

The other profile showed that Dee Brandison was indeed a beautiful woman, in her very early thirties, he thought. But she would carry that scar to her grave.

Santee was glad he had killed Olly Patch. 'Sorry I didn't shoot him sooner, Brandy.'

Her good eye — a shade of blue that went well with her flaxen hair — studied him as he sat down in the only bedside chair. The room was very feminine and it made Santee uncomfortable, as if he had no right being here, among such pink and pale-yellow fripperies adorning the walls and windows, the heady perfume, and the blue silk gown with its butterfly embroidery draped over the end of the bed.

'Carey said you work for the governor.' Her voice was soft, and although he couldn't see her body beneath the bedclothes he could easily savvy how she was the most popular whore in the Butterfly House. To some of her lonely, younger customers she might even seem a mother-figure, or perhaps a big sister. Her speech was slightly slurred now, because of the mild concussion, he guessed.

'I work for Governor Burdin, and my job here is to find out who killed Josh Rankin, and why. I think mebbe I know why now.' He waited but she said nothing. 'But I'm wonderin' how, and why, Josh came to you.'

She gave him a sober look, then smiled faintly. 'I know about Deborah. Josh didn't visit me for the usual reasons. Carey, in his job as deputy, found him drunk and feeling terribly sorry for himself in one of the alleys near here. My brother is a kind-hearted man, and he saw Josh had a real problem he was trying to drown in booze. He thought I might be able to help him.'

Santee frowned. 'In what way?' he asked stiffly.

She laughed aloud, clapping a hand swiftly to the swollen side of her face. 'Oh! Please don't make me laugh! You — you look so outraged! I'm a good listener, Mr Santee: believe it or not, it's one of the secrets of being a successful whore.' She seemed to have no problem with calling herself that. 'Josh was too sick and sorry for himself to have anything else on his mind but his own troubles and, I suspect, he had a very low opinion of himself and was worried about returning to Deborah after what had happened.'

Santee had an idea what she was

saying but decided to leave it right there.

'From what Carey told me, it seems while I was off on a wild goose chase, Josh found the man who'd' — he searched for the word, annoyed that he should feel tongue-tied with her.

She said, huskily, small hands holding the edge of the sheet tightly, 'Defiled him?'

Santee nodded jerkily, still uneasy with this subject. 'Yeah, I think mebbe it started out as a prank but somehow got out of hand. I'm sure Josh had been beaten up but he wouldn't admit it. I know he could fight pretty good: his father had him taught pugilism by some Limey ex-champion, so I reckon it would've taken a few men to hold him while he was beaten, and then . . . '

Her single eye watched him and he was surprised to see a faint smile on those full red lips. 'No need for embarrassment, Mr Santee, I'm familiar with this subject, as you must realize, being in the trade I follow. I don't like it, but I can talk frankly if need be.'

Santee squirmed. 'OK! We both know what we're talking about. And we both knew Josh. I'm not sure any longer who knew him best, but — did he tell you anything at all about what had happened?'

She was silent for so long he thought she wasn't going to reply and then she nodded and he was startled to see her brush a tear away from her good eye. '*He told me everything*!' she said huskily, then seemed to make an effort to keep herself under control. 'It just spilled out of him. That poor boy! So innocent, so desperate to — to *learn* and belong. He wanted nothing more than to be accepted as a man of the frontier. He admired the men who lived so hard and worked — and played — so hard, wanted to be like them. Then to be confronted by someone who was perverted. No wonder it shattered him. The experience as well as the shock of realizing that — well, that it takes all kinds to make this world we live in, even out here.'

'I'd already figured that out — without knowing the details.' Santee spoke more curtly than he meant to, still feeling uneasy. 'What I want to know is who set him up, and what Josh tried to do about it.'

'Obviously, he was totally devastated, and felt dreadful shame, though he could hardly be blamed for what had happened. After breaking down and pouring out his very soul to me, he said he planned to exact a very fitting and completely merciless vengeance. He knew it was a major task, could even be beyond him, but he was determined not to ask for help. As he saw it, this was his chore, and his alone. I suspect he was thinking of his . . . standing with you . . . and the so-called frontier code, that a real man fights his own battles. *Which is rubbish, of course!*' She paused. 'I think he regarded it as his entry into what he believed to be manhood out here. He was very naïve,

Mr Santee — and also very stubborn.'

'What all that fancy talk comes down to is he aimed to find the man and kill him. Right?'

Santee's flat statement brought her up short and words she had been about to speak died on her lips.

'Exactly what you would've done, I believe . . . You were more of a model for him than perhaps you knew.'

He merely stared back steadily, deadpan, and, for a moment she was the one who was unnerved.

'The cowboys he had been drinking with — and they made *sure* he was well plied with liquor, maybe even spiked it with something — took him down to the river where the man was waiting. Josh was very drunk and slow to see what was happening.' She paused again. 'You were right. It seems four or five held him, while the *man* beat him. Then, while he was unconscious — '

'All right! It's about how I figured it. All I need now is the name of this son of a bitch.'

'Josh didn't know it, except for Whitey — everyone was careful not to call him anything else. In fact, they all seemed to tread very warily around him.' She gave a small shudder. 'He sounds very frightening — perhaps even unbalanced.'

Whitey. It had to be the fair-haired man who had committed the actual murder, seen by the mystery girl and Navajo Joe through the screening bushes.

'They left him there, and he eventually made his way back to Phoenix where he was supposed to meet you.'

'Yeah. I was arranging for him to inspect some more herds, but he wasn't interested. I savvy now why he'd lost interest in everything except tracking down the scum who'd set him up.' He sighed. 'I wish to hell he'd told me!'

'I think he was too ashamed, you being so . . . manly and — ' He glared and she saw he was both hurt and puzzled. 'You were supposed to be his bodyguard, perhaps a little more. I had the impression he saw you as a close friend, a man he'd like to emulate.'

'Well, I don't shape up too good in that department,' He couldn't hide the bitterness and she regarded him with a different light in her one visible blue eye.

'Forgive my surprise, Mr Santee, but I don't meet many men with a genuine conscience.'

He covered by building a cigarette and lighting it. She watched his every movement. 'Name's Jim.'

'I think you could be a very interesting man to talk to, Jim Santee. Are you planning on staying in Phoenix for a while?'

He stood, shaking his head. 'Not unless the men I'm looking for are still around here. Did Josh mention their names? Where they came from, or how he came to meet them?'

'I had the impression he already knew them.'

'He couldn't've. He'd never been here before. We looked for ranches that had good breeding stock and . . . ' He let the rest run off. 'If they were cowpokes from one of those ranches, though, and he met up with them in a saloon — and they filled him with liquor, figuring to play a prank . . . '

'Yes, it could've been that way,' she agreed, though she frowned slightly. 'Still, it seems too well planned for some chance thing.'

He agreed quietly, but thought to himself that it could be that this Whitey was waiting in the wings for the cowhands to bring him some likely victim and perhaps not for the first time.

'Reckon I've learnt as much as I can from you, Brandy. Except — how about Eddie Bale? Why did he run to you?'

She was sober now. 'Poor Eddie. A very lonely man and his profession did nothing to help him feel less lonely, He was regarded with scarcely concealed scorn by almost everyone he knew, being a prison guard.'

'But not by you.'

The blue eyes were cool as they sought his face. 'I told you, I'm a good listener. Some time back Eddie visited me, maudlin, and he admitted his loneliness and feeling of inadequacy. I felt sorry for him.' A smile flashed briefly. 'One of my failings, according to Carey! Well, I listened sympathetically, agreed with him where I thought it would help and I think the poor man fell in love with me.'

Santee could see how it might happen, though he hadn't figured Bale for that kind. Still, having someone as beautiful as Brandy on your side — it must have been mighty comforting for someone as unhappy as Bale.

'I made it very clear from the beginning that there could be nothing between us, but Eddie seemed happy enough with things just as they were. I told him I didn't want him as a customer any more and all he did was smile.'

'Why did he come to you this time?'

She sobered. 'He was afraid. He'd

seen something in the prison he wasn't supposed to. He thought they might kill him, so he asked for leave and never intended to go back.'

'He say what it was that spooked him?'

'He'd been drinking. Something about a man drowning in a river after falling off a wall. But he said it was no accident: the man was *thrown* off. He was afraid that if someone realized he'd seen the crime, he might be killed, too. So he ran, wanted me to go away with him.'

'Figured it might be something like that. Well, I can figure out who sent Olly Patch, but it doesn't help me find this Whitey.'

'I'm afraid I can't help you there, either.'

'You've helped plenty, Brandy, and I'm much obliged.' He stood, hitching at his gunbelt. 'And don't worry about that scar. You're too handsome a woman for a little thing like that to put men off.'

'Why, thank you, Jim! I never

expected such a compliment from you. Will you come to see me again?'

But he was already moving out of the room, his breathing constricted, and he knew deep down it wasn't just the feminine decor that had caused his unease.

Brandy was quite a woman and, being honest with himself, he admitted it had taken a deal of will-power to stay focused on the subject he had come to discuss.

Now it was time to concentrate on tracking down this Whitey and his friends — and bury the sons of bitches before too many more suns had set behind the Buckeye Range.

* * *

Sheriff Kelly Sanchez was standing on his law office landing as Santee rode slowly by, lightly touching a hand to his hatbrim. Sanchez merely checked the watch he held and glanced up, deadpan. Santee laughed.

'Mebbe see you again, Sheriff.'

'Not if I see you first.'

Santee rode on, feeling Sanchez' gaze boring into his back. The man was clearly obsessed with creating a good impression on the townsfolk and he figured it was because of his Mexican blood. He sympathized a little: he had been through a similar time long time ago, before he decided to hell with people: they took him as he was or not at all.

So far it had worked well enough.

The river-bank seemed the most logical place to begin, though he didn't expect to find any clues, not after all this time. But he would be able to get the feel of the place: the Sioux had taught him how important that could be when on a vengeance hunt.

It was a pleasant enough spot, grassy, brush-clad, clumps of trees, difficult to get to: he would not have found it except Carey had privately checked it out after hearing Josh's story, though he had done nothing about it.

The place was just outside Sanchez's jurisdiction, and being a stickler for the rule book, the sheriff had no interest.

Ideal place for what had happened! Santee thought grimly. *Shielded like this from prying eyes.*

He found scuffed places, one at the edge of the trees where the horses had been tethered. Studying it, he felt the ground with his fingertips: slightly moist because the grass was thick and lush, ideal for holding sign — and there hadn't been any heavy rain recently. So he found hoofprints of at least five riders — maybe one set had been made by Whitey's horse. He took his time, separating the prints and settled on six riders; one lot would have been made by Josh Rankin, one by Whitey, the rest by the riders who had set things up and gotten Josh into the bind he'd found himself in.

They either had a twisted sense of humour, or — recalling Brandy's assessment of how Josh had described things, or what he could remember of them — this had all been prearranged and they were doing *Whitey*'s bidding, possibly not for the first time.

He wondered what had happened to other victims — if there had been any?

The hoofprints gave him some idea of how many he was up against. And he had noted that at least three sets of shoes showed similar markings on the metal — made by the same blacksmith, the hammerblows in the same places; either square on or skidding off slightly, the curve at an angle the blacksmith favoured, which meant riders from the same ranch.

There were several other places where the grass was still scuffed and trampled: maybe where Josh was beaten, dragged off a little way to where Whitey waited . . .

That was as far as he allowed his thoughts to go.

He took his notebook out of his saddle-bags, running down the list of ranches where they had purchased breeding cattle or had at least examined them.

Five spreads within thirty miles of here. He had a deal of riding to do — and he carried a clear picture of those similar hoofmarks in his head.

He would know them immediately.

And the man who was riding the horse that made them had better be able to explain how and when he had left those prints on this river-bank.

8

Raising Hell

He watched the men near the rear door, outside the lineshack, preparing their supper. They were cooking on a slab of sheet metal across a couple of rocks, between which a small fire burned. It smelled like venison steaks and his mouth was full of saliva as he brought the rifle slowly to his shoulder.

The first shot lifted the hot plate, scattering the sizzling steaks and grease and stale bread that was frying. The cook, squatting, heaved backwards with a startled yell. The second man, setting a coffee pot over a smaller fire, spun quickly, dropping the pot. An instant later it sailed and spun through the air, trailing coffee grinds and water before smashing into the side of the lineshack.

They were on the ground and rolling,

looking wildly about them, groping for their guns now.

Santee raked the area around them with three shots, sending them cowering from the eruptions of dirt and stones. They made for the low step up into the shack itself, half dragging, half crouched, staggering and stumbling, scared and shocked, both trying to squeeze through the narrow dorway at the same time.

He let them get inside and when they slammed the plank door, emptied the rifle into it, splinters flying. From inside came yells and the shattering of china or glass, the clattering of overturned chairs as the men scrabbled for cover.

'Who the hell is that?' one of them called, voice frantic.

The other fired a wild shot beneath a window shutter that had jammed part-way open. It was no more than token resistance.

Santee reloaded unhurriedly. When the magazine was full he fired three times into the rusted chimney. It crumpled and twisted, a length breaking off and clattering as it rolled down the shingled roof. More shots lifted a line of those shingles and sent them spinning, exposing the old tarpaper underneath.

The cowboys both fired back now, wild shots, likely just crouching below the windows and holding the Colts up and triggering.

'*Who the hell are you?*' The same hoarse voice as earlier.

'*Who are you?*' countered Santee.

'Judas! You dunno whose place this is? Hell, man, you're in a lot of trouble! This is Heath Dakin's north lineshack! *Heath Dakin!* That mean anythin' to you, you dummy?'

'Yeah, he ran me off the spread this morning. Him and half-a-dozen hardcases.'

'Then you must be loco, shootin' us up!'

This was the second man, outraged, but still with a tremor of fear in his voice.

'Aw, just thought I'd let Heath know I'm still around. Fact, you tell him I'll be back every night to shoot-up your lineshack — and a few of his others, too.'

'Christ man, you *are* loco!'

'Sure must be eager to die!'

Santee emptied the rifle into the shack, shooting the strut out from under the jammed window shutter, raking the side door, holing the tin bowls on the wash bench — and the water keg standing strapped to a rear corner.

'*Judas! Will you quit it?*'

'For now. Got some other chores to do tonight. Now you boys be sure to tell Heath Dakin that I'll be hanging about for a while. When I get tired of it, I'm coming for him. You tell him that — *Buenas noches, amigos*. See you in the morning.'

★　★　★

Santee smiled to himself as he lay in knee-deep grass on the edge of the big holding pasture. There was a lot of activity there, low curses that were not all directed at the skittish mounts or the bustling cattle.

The nighthawks were being doubled and the hands called to extra duty were not happy. So he figured at least one of the men in the north lineshack had ridden down to tell Dakin that Santee was still around and raising hell.

'He won't get within a mile of this herd tonight.' The words came drifting in with the gentle night wind and he smiled to himself. *Someone was over-confident.*

We'll see, boys . . .

He eased back onto the slight slope and slid down the slippery grass to the hollow where he had left his mount.

'Remember,' a voice called from above — he thought he recognized it as Dakin's tough ramrod, Whit Gant. 'Shoot on sight — but for Chris' sakes make sure of your target!'

Seemed like Dakin was some rattled, which could mean he knew a lot more than he admitted to. Or was he just riled that a man like Santee was openly defying him?

Well, Heath Dakin hadn't seen anything yet.

Leading his mount, Santee made his way along the draw below the big pasture. He watched the skyline, but nothing moved against the stars on this side. They would be concentrating on the other three sides that faced the hills and wild country: no one would believe he was already between the outlying pastures and the main house.

Crouching, moving slowly, he searched for his landmark — a dead tree jutting out at a thirty-degree angle. He recognized its shape against the stars and moved in, leaving the reins trailing.

He had a large box of kitchen-sized vestas — *144 Surefire Lights*, according to the label. Crouched double, leg a little stiff, he crabbed his way to the edge of a natural run-off carved by past rainstorms. He had piled dead grass and twigs about three yards in from the edge, trailed a 'fuse' of more dead grass and leaves to where he was now.

Cattle moved and snorted restively several yards away as they sought a place to settle for the night.

Using his body as a shield, he struck one of the four-inch long wooden-stemmed matches. It flared and he quickly thrust it into the 'fuse' trail. Even as it crackled he tossed the slightly open box of the remaining 143 large vestas into the piled grass. When the small fire from the grass trail reached that it would flare like a rocket, spook the herd and set the stacked deadwood ablaze.

Someone spotted the burning trail of grass and yelled, but it was too late. The vesta box went up with a *whoosh!* leaping almost a foot into the air, spewing blazing vestas in a wide arc.

'Fire! Jesus! Fire! *Fire*!'

Panic had already set in. The cattle bawled. Horns clashed. The cattle bawled louder. He felt the first tremors through the earth as the herd gathered and started to prowl, bellowing — then the muted thunder of the beginning of the stampede. Men yelled. Hoofs rattled over the hard earth. Cattle bellowed endlessly. A horse shrilled and a rider screamed as he was thrown into the moving river of steers.

Someone panicked and fired two shots, earning blistering curses and oaths from Gant.

'Goddammit! You think they ain't already spooked enough!'

The fire had taken hold of the pasture now and the stampede wouldn't stop this side of the Great Divide, Santee reckoned. *Time he was somewhere else.*

He smiled crookedly, mounted and rode away — the frantic cowboys were too damn busy to even notice as he turned slowly towards the lights of the distant ranch house.

The fire was easily visible and there were a few people on the porch of the big log-and-riverstone house. He figured one of the men would be Dakin himself. As if to confirm the thought, Dakin's voice snapped as he turned to the tall, dark shape beside him: a tall, dark shape with light-coloured hair!

Whit Gant, the Flying D ramrod. They had met that morning and the man had obviously been disappointed that Dakin had prevented him from shooting Santee on the spot. *A big, tall man with light-coloured hair* — that was how Navajo Joe had described the man who had murdered Josh Rankin.

This morning, Gant had had his hat on and Santee hadn't noticed his hair — from what he could see now as the man passed through a slant of dull light angling from the front door of the house, the hair was a light gold.

By God! Did that qualify him for the nickname Whitey?

Gant was yelling orders in a deep voice, the other men who had been on the porch running towards the corrals. Dakin, himself in shadow, stayed on the porch and watched the flames leaping up from the south pasture, heard the diminishing thunder of a stampede, the occasional gunshot as someone tried to turn steers in all-out panic.

'You be all right here, boss?' Gant was back, hat jammed back on his head, a rifle in his hand.

'Get moving!' growled Dakin. 'You see that 'breed, you bring him in to me alive — I don't care if he's got some lead in him, or he's had a kickin', but I want him *alive*!'

'I'll get him, boss.'

Dakin watched his men thunder out of the yard. There were lights burning in the large bunkhouse, but the doors were open and it was clear the place was empty. Even the cook had been despatched to help stop the stampede and put out the fire.

Santee waited a short time, made sure his horse was properly ground-hitched this time — he wanted to know he would find it exactly where it was supposed to be when it was time for him to quit the Flying D.

Then he checked his Colt and made

his way to the house, keeping to shadows of the outbuildings, reaching the kitchen door without trouble. He smelled the remains of the supper. There were lights burning in a hallway where several small portraits of a woman hung on the walls. The parlour had two lamps burning and, as he padded across, he noticed a lot of small picture frames bunched together on a sideboy — containing tintypes of the woman in the hall. Most of the frames looked like silver, though a few were polished wood. He looked at her and a younger Dakin in an obvious wedding picture. They appeared together in other tintypes, sometimes with one, two or three children — two boys and a girl, at various ages. At what he took to be a later time, there was only the younger boy and girl — the other son, older and tow-headed, was no longer in any of the pictures.

It had distracted him for a few seconds, now he saw light in another room off to one side. Dakin's shadow moved about in there, and he heard the clink of a bottle neck against a glass rim.

He went silently to the door. The rancher was sitting in a padded chair at a large, paper-strewn mahogany desk with gold-leaf patterns edging the dark green leather of the desktop. There were two embossed silver frames and the woman — Dakin's wife, Santee had decided — was in both: head and shoulders, one with a hat, the other smiling and bareheaded, showing a lot of blond hair. Average looks.

Dakin was seated behind his desk, nursing a glass of whiskey, a medium-sized man, in his fifties, with a crabby face and tight mouth. He had the look of a man who would remember the first dollar he had ever made — and how much of it he had spent and on what.

Of course, these days his dollars were counted in the hundreds of thousands. Which fact counted with a mighty lot of people, both within Arizona and neighbouring states or territories, even clear across the country to Washington.

To Jim Santee, it counted for exactly nothing.

He had never stood in awe of men who held themselves aloof, considered themselves to be richer and more powerful, better than other men, deserving of more respect.

So there was no hesitation now as he walked into the startled Dakin's office, saying, 'Let's take up where we left off this morning, Dakin — OK with you?'

The rancher had spilled his drink, let the glass drop, made a belated lunge for a half-open desk drawer. Two long strides took Santee to the desk and he kicked the drawer closed, narrowly missing jamming Dakin's fingers.

'What the hell're you doing here?' There was no fear in those cold grey eyes and the lips had compressed to a razor slash in the flat, oval face. He was nursing one hand.

'Look out the window and see.'

'I know what you've done, curse you! And don't think you'll leave Flying D land alive this time!'

'Well, we'll see,' Santee toed out a straightback chair and dropped into it, angled so he could watch the door. He held his gun loosely across his legs. 'You were a mite too quick getting rid of me this morning, Dakin.'

'Not quick enough you ask me. Should've put a bullet in you.'

Santee smiled thinly. 'Now where's all that big-smilin', come-on-up-to-my-house-an'-have-a-drink welcome gone? Heath, ol' son, you are being two-faced over this and I figure it has to be because you got a guilty conscience.'

The bleak eyes seemed to snap at him. 'You figure wrong. I was interested in sellin' my breeder cows when you first showed with young Rankin — that's what all the smilin' and drink-offerin' was about — but you know that well as I do. Since then, you've had a slew of trouble and the boy's dead — in an ugly way, I hear. I can't afford to get mixed-up in anythin' like that! Man, I know your governor well enough to call him by his first name. I number senators among my friends and drinking companions. I have grown-up children back East, movin' in circles that'll take them into high society and give 'em contacts that'll set 'em up for life!' He threw out his arms, 'I have three ranches like this, own more herds in Wyoming. You think I want to be connected to some sordid murder on a damn sandspit?'

'Seems we live in different worlds, Dakin. When you get right down to it, I'm no more than a gunfighter working for the governor. But I take my job seriously and it was to guard Josh Rankin while he bought breeding cattle for his new business, backed by his father. Now Josh's dead: which means I didn't do my job properly and I aim to set that to rights. I don't care if I tread on the toes of the King of England, or muddy-up the skirts of the Queen of Russia, but I *will* get it done. Upsettin' you won't even make me miss a draw on my cigarette.'

Dakin's eyes narrowed. 'I knew when I first laid eyes on you that you'd be the one to cause me trouble! Goddamnit I *knew* it! I had a feelin' — that same hunch that has gotten me right through to where I am now, mister, and I tell you, I don't aim to move one goddamn inch!'

'Dakin, you're diggin' your grave deeper every time you open your mouth. You didn't gimme time to explain anything this morning. Soon as I showed, you set your dogs on me. Now, just sit still and shut up for a minute! I'll tie you up and gag you if you don't.'

'I'd like to see you try!' scoffed the rancher, but there wasn't much confidence in his protest.

Santee smiled crookedly. 'Could be you'll get your chance. Someone bushwhacked me north of Phoenix. Several riders, three or four. I reckon I winged at least one. I didn't look very hard at their tracks because they'd lit-out and were set to hit Texas before they reined-down. I went back to the river-bank where Josh met some trouble and I found several sets of hoof-prints: some of 'em matched at least one set of the *hombres* who'd drygulched me.'

'What's that got to do with me?'

'They were *distinctive* hoofprints, certain hammer marks in the metal all the same, nail holes staggered a little. I found tracks to match at your gate and in that front pasture — which is about where you sent Gant and his pards down to see me on my way.'

'Hell, that proves nothing!'

'Does — 'cause I got me a look in your forge and found sets of horse-shoes, all with those same marks on 'em — your smith is the man who made those shoes.'

Dakin frowned slightly, was silent, and Santee let it drag on. The sounds of the stampede were fading outside. He had one ear cocked for returning riders, hand holding the Colt more firmly now.

Dakin hadn't failed to notice. 'Wait a minute — you're not only sayin' some of my men tried to ambush you, but that they were mixed up in Josh Rankin's killing?'

'Well, it's a big jump from the river-bank to that, but it's possible — unless you can convince me otherwise.'

'Damn you, Santee! You should've stayed with the Sioux! You'd make a good Injun — and the only good Injuns I know are dead! But you don't rattle me! I've no intention of trying to convince you of anything. But, I'll say this: Flying D has a reputation up this way for producing top hands and mounting them on fine broncs — with mighty good shoes! Word got around years ago about those horseshoes, and my blacksmith — man named Three-hole Macreedy, 'cause he never makes more than three holes in the inside arm of his horseshoes.'

Santee admitted quietly he had heard of Macreedy, and not just locally, but way up north and to the east as well. The man's expertise was widespread.

'All right. With my full permission, Mac runs a side business selling his shoes all over the country — check with the Painted Rock Trading Company if you want — they handle the shipping side of it for him and keep his books.'

Santee had to believe the man. It was in the moon-face, and the tone: Dakin was full of confidence, and now a touch of the old arrogance was back as well, for he knew he had Santee beat.

'So, you want to trace the riders of the broncs go right ahead, but you'll still be doin' it the other side of Christmas! Those shoes are sold over half the country.'

'You could be right, Dakin, but the tracks I found were made by riders from around here. So the rest of the country don't count.'

Dakin stared at him a long time, poured himself another drink without offering one to Santee. 'Agin the law to give booze to Injuns, ain't it?' he said slyly, but Santee didn't answer. The rancher drank, looking over the rim of his glass. 'Now why would any men of mine want to cause young Josh so much trouble? You can't answer, can you?'

'Your men are pranksters, like every damn ranch crew I've ever met — 'specially if there's a greenhorn within spittin' distance. And Josh was green as they come — Naïve, sure, but added to that was his enthusiasm and eagerness to be accepted by real, dyed-in-the-wool cowboys. That was all he wanted. So he was willing to go along with their crazy dares and pranks, even if he knew he could come out badly. It was worth it to him as long as they thought he was a good sport.'

Dakin was frowning deeply now. 'You're talkin' double-Dutch with a hatful of French throwed in far as I'm concerned.'

'Your men got him drunk, set him up for a prank that went wrong. I'm guessing, but I don't think they meant it to turn out quite the way it did . . . If I thought different, you'd have a lot of dead men on your crew by now.'

Dakin, for the first time — maybe the first time ever — looked uncertain, almost lost. He seemed about to speak but remained silent as Santee continued.

'First of all, is Gant ever called Whitey?'

Santee sat straighter in his chair, gun half-cocked now as he planted his boots firmly on the floor and tensed. Dakin's reaction had startled him. The rancher had half-risen, gripping the edge of the desktop as if he would snap it off, the colour draining from his face.

'Wh-what d'you know about Whitey?'

Santee considered his reply a long moment. 'He murdered Josh. I've heard he's very tall and has pale hair. Kind of fits Whit Gant . . . And if Whit's short for Whitney it's not too much of a jump to Whitey.'

'Well, you're wrong!' snapped Heath Dakin, his eyes burning now, knuckles white around his glass. 'No one calls Gant *Whitey* — no one calls him anythin' but Whit, unless they're cussin'

165

him and a man'd need to be tired of livin' to cuss-out Whit Gant.'

Santee relaxed a little. 'Mebbe so — but the name Whitey means something to you.'

'Not a damn thing!' Dakin told him quickly, giving him a bold and steady stare.

'You're a liar.' A cold, flat accusation and Santee was ready for any kind of reaction it provoked.

But Dakin, nostrils flared, face murderous, swallowed his rage and shook his head slowly, easing back into his chair. 'No,' was all he said, huskily.

Santee was *sure* the man was lying: his reaction at the first mention of the name was enough to convince him. But he had no chance to follow it through.

The window behind him shattered. He went forward out of the chair, twisting so he came half-around on one knee, cocked pistol raised. But he held his fire.

He was looking into the yawning twin barrels of a shotgun, a man's head and shoulders silhouetted behind.

Whit Gant's deep voice said, 'Drop it, 'breed! Or don't. Mine's the second choice, but you make up your own mind — in about half a second. 'Cause that's all you got.'

9

Pow-Wow

That was all Santee needed: he remembered a voice on the front porch of this house not long ago: '*You bring him in alive! I don't care if he's got a bullet in him, or he's had a kickin'* — *as long as he's alive!*'

So Gant wouldn't shoot, not with orders like that — *he hoped!*

Santee fired, throwing himself flat as the shotgun barrels tilted upwards violently and discharged. Dust and laths and rubbish from the roof space rained down onto the desk and sent Dakin diving for the floor. He reached a shaking hand up towards the drawer that held the pistol.

Santee fired again and the man howled, snatching back his blood-spurting arm, rolling into the clear.

From outside came a wild yell.

'Judas! He got Gant!'

'Find out who that is and how many there are!' Santee gritted, holding his smoking Colt on the wounded Dakin. '*Do it*!'

The rancher glared but saw something in Santee's eyes, cleared his throat and called, 'How bad is he, Salty?'

'Head shot! Judas — blood everywhere. You all right, boss?'

'No, he's not all right!' Santee called back. 'He's wounded and he'll die if you *hombres* get froggy — Drag Gant in here.'

'Gawd almighty, he's a damn *tree*!'

'Get some help — and leave your guns behind. How many are you?' There was a hesitation and Santee knew the man would lie to him.

'Just me an' Tolliver.'

'Then you and Tolliver bring in Dakin. The rest of you get the hell back to the bunkhouse, close all the windows and doors — ' He reached forward and prodded Dakin as the man twisted his face in pain. 'Tell 'em!'

Dakin swallowed. 'Do like he says, boys. He's loco — he'll shoot me up slowly unless I miss my guess.'

'That's a good guess,' Santee assured him coldly.

There were murmurings and scufflings outside the broken window and, in a few minutes, two bedraggled cowboys — sweaty and scratched-up from their ride to stop the stampede and extinguish the pasture fire — staggered in with a bloody-faced Whit Gant sagging between them. The man was either passed-out or dead.

It didn't matter a hell of a lot to Santee, either way right now.

At a gesture from his gun barrel they set him down against the wall at the end of the desk. Dakin was slumped in his chair now, using his good hand to pick the picture frames out of the mess the shotgun had brought down on his desk. He blew the dust off each, swore softly when he saw broken glass in one. He set them upright before making an attempt to wrap a bandanna around his bleeding arm.

'Lend a hand here, Salty!'

The smallest cowboy, a dried-out veteran of the range, watched Santee warily as he went to help his boss. The other cowboy, Tolliver, was rangy and bearded. He looked a lot tougher than Salty.

'See what you can do for Gant,' ordered Santee, leaning casually against the wall now, gun fully loaded again and already cocked. Tolliver threw him a hard look and went towards a cupboard. 'Open it mighty carefully, feller.'

'It's just — medical things.' Dakin was a little breathless now, the shock of his arm wound starting to reach him.

Santee watched as the rancher and his ramrod were roughly doctored by the cowboys.

He stayed out of line with the window, using the corner shadows, listening for furtive movements outside the house. He could see part of the bunkhouse from one corner through the window and it was in darkness — which didn't mean the men had obeyed his orders and closed themselves in.

He had the upper hand right now, but there was a lot of Flying D outside, between him and his ground-hitched mount: a lot of Dakin's land, and a lot of Dakin's riders.

Whatever he found out — or didn't — wouldn't be much use to him if he couldn't get away with a whole hide.

Gant stirred, only moaning a little, but at least it indicated he was still alive. *He might hold the answer . . .*

Somebody better.

Dakin's arm was in a rough sling now. Gant looked pale and his face was streaked with blood that Tolliver hadn't quite managed to wipe away. The rangy cowboy stood close to Gant's sprawled form, watching Santee closely. Salty sat on one edge of the desk near his boss, looking worried.

'You can't get away, feller,' he said hoarsely.

'Give Gant some of that whiskey.'

Salty looked startled, glanced at Dakin who nodded wearily. Pain was getting to him and he didn't want it to fog up his mind right now. He glanced at the two photo frames and the handsome woman's face staring back at him. Then he raised his pain-dulled eyes to Santee.

'I can't help you, Injun. I know nothing about how Josh Rankin died. If any of my men had anythin' to do with it, you can have 'em — but I'll back 'em all the way, if they deny it.'

'You're still a liar.' Santee's words made Tolliver stiffen, his big calloused hands clenching into fists. Jim swivelled his gaze to the man. 'You got somethin' to say?'

'Yeah — you ain't gonna live much longer.'

Santee smiled crookedly. 'Where've I heard that before . . . ? Mebbe you were one of the fools who dared Josh into drinking way too much, then set him up with this son of a bitch they call Whitey.'

Santee swivelled his gaze to Dakin as he said it, deliberately trying to provoke a reaction. But the rancher was fighting down his pain, maintaining control with an effort, and he met Santee's gaze, shrugged.

'You got some sort of thing about this Whitey. You know who he means, Salty? Tolliver?'

Both shook their heads, Salty licking his lips, Tolliver looking malevolent. *Dangerous bastard*, Santee allowed to himself.

'Get Gant that whiskey, damnit! I wanna talk to him.'

Salty had been fiddling with the bottle, now jumped, sloshed a good shot into the glass and knelt beside Gant, forcing the rim between his lips. Gant coughed and spluttered, thrashed weakly, one arm knocking the glass from Salty's grip. The old cowboy looked anxiously over his shoulder at Santee.

Jim jerked his gun barrel. 'Stand aside.'

He watched Gant slowly come out of it, face etched with pain, the man squinting, grunting once. He blinked, trying to focus, gaze passing over Dakin to end at Santee.

'Shoulda . . . just . . . blasted you,' he rasped.

'It's all right, Whit, you followed orders. Sorry it nearly got you killed.' Dakin sounded genuine in his concern for his big, tough ramrod. 'At the risk of boring you, Injun, Salty's right: you won't get off Flying D alive.'

'I don't, then you die first.'

It was said casually but with a chill that made Salty actually shudder. Dakin went very still. Tolliver's expression or stance didn't change, and Gant frowned, winced, obviously in pain.

There was a silence, broken occasionally by a grunt of pain from Gant or Salty sniffing loudly. There were no sounds from outside but Santee knew Dakin's men would be out there, waiting with cocked guns.

'Dakin, you and me leave together.

I'd like to question Gant a lot more, but he's too damn big to drag along.' He nodded once at the foreman. Gant's eyes closed involuntarily now as the pain from the head wound worked on him. 'You got anything you'd like to volunteer, Gant? Or should I call you Whitey?'

He threw that in for one reason only: to catch Dakin off guard. The rancher stiffened but straightened his face quickly and shook his head.

'You're a damn fool, Santee. We dunno who this Whitey is. Sure you got the name right?'

Santee didn't bother to answer. He knew that Dakin was trying to cover but hadn't quite pulled it off.

'On your feet, Heath.'

Dakin stiffened but made no move to get out of his chair. 'Now just a minute! I'm not going anywhere with you.'

'Then stay — but they'll have to bury you.' Santee thumbed the hammer, let them see his finger bring the trigger all the way back: if the hammer spur slipped from under his thumb now, Dakin was dead.

The rancher was rigid. He ran a tongue around his lips. Salty was wide-eyed, Tolliver tensed, ready to spring like a hunting cougar. Gant lifted a hand briefly and let it flop back.

'All right, Santee. S'pose some of our boys did meet Josh Rankin and had a little fun . . . ?'

'Shut up, Whit!'

'It's OK, boss. You hear me, Santee? But not *just* our boys. Slocum was prowlin', too, with his Gila Bend bunch, lookin' to raise some hell. Whatever they done was only meant as a prank. The kid was ripe for some raggin'. No one here knows who this Whitey feller is — how he come to butt-in, beats me. But he must've — and after our boys left. So you got no beef with Flyin' D.'

'That's the way you see it, Gant?'

'It's the way it has to be. I wasn't there, dunno which of the boys were, even. But I know these rannies. They'll push a prank all the way but they'll draw the line at anyone gettin' badly hurt — let alone killed.'

'There were three or four cowboys with this Whitey when he murdered Josh. Every one of 'em joined in brutalizing the woman who witnessed Josh's murder . . . '

'Hell! They wouldn't be our men!' Gant said, his vehemence making him grab at his head, his face contorted. He looked through his spread fingers at Santee. 'I dunno of one man on our crew who'd have anythin' to do with murder an' rape — '

Dakin was quick to add, 'Nor do I!'

Jim Santee's eyes flicked from one to the other. 'You're both liars.'

'Slocum's bunch are scum — ' Dakin began. Then —

'Hey, in there!' a rough voice called suddenly. 'You, 'breed, whoever you are. We got this place surrounded. You can't take one step outside without stoppin' lead. You wanna call it quits while you're still breathin'?'

'No need. I've got your boss. He'll be first to die.'

'An' you'll be second! It ain't no good, feller. Forget about takin' hostages; you're already dead unless you give up and the boss comes out unharmed.'

'I'll go along with that, Rusty!' Dakin called, a look of triumph on his face as he glanced at Santee. 'You do what you have to, but don't let this son of a bitch ride out of here!' He leered at Santee. 'Now, your move, Injun!'

Santee merely nodded, strode across to stand behind Dakin's chair and placed the gun muzzle in his right ear. The rancher sucked in a long, audible breath, half rising.

'Sure you don't want to change that order?'

Dakin, obviously strung-out and as near to being scared as he would allow to show, shook his head slightly, breath hissing through his nostrils now. Santee reached down, grabbed a handful of the man's shirt and hauled him roughly to his feet. The rancher grunted in pain as his wounded arm brushed the edge of the desk, slumped over involuntarily.

Santee stumbled, caught unawares as the man's weight suddenly dragged at his arm.

Tolliver made his move.

He launched himself in a headlong dive across the desk, knocking Salty off with a yell, and the cowboy fell on top of Gant who squirmed and shouted. Dakin was sent sprawling and knocked Santee into the wall. His gun blasted and Tolliver staggered, but managed to slam a knotted fist against Santee's jaw. Jim floundered, shooting again, knowing it was wild, but figuring any kind of a shot would help him right now. Tolliver seemed to be all over him, sledging and hooking with leather-hard fists.

Santee, nose bleeding, jaw throbbing, swung his smoking gun up at Tolliver's head. The man sagged but caught the edge of the big desk and kept from going down all the way. Salty started to move in, but Santee threw the table lamp at him. It missed, hit the wall, glass shattering and hot oil igniting as it spewed out.

Gant began to yell. 'I'm on fire! I'm on fire!'

He tried to beat at his trousers as flames ate into them. The oil spread and flared up under a curtain. Dakin grabbed it and hauled it down. It fell across his desk and the piled papers there caught instantly.

Dakin was yelling 'Fire!' now, too, and Tolliver was still going after Santee, who smashed his gun into the cowboy's face. Tolliver was felled by the blow this time and Santee untangled his feet from the man's tumbling body, reaching for Dakin. Salty had thrown a floor rug over Gant's legs, extinguishing the flames.

But Dakin only wanted to save his ranch, was hurling piles of burning papers to the floor, stamping frantically on them. Then the door burst open and armed cowboys swept in. Santee shot out the remaining lamp, but the leaping flames still illuminated the scene in weird bursts of light alternating with flowing pools of blackness. Someone started shooting and men scattered — this place was too confined for random gunfire.

Santee ducked under the burning desk and Gant, his trousers no longer aflame, made a half-hearted grab at him. Jim hooked an elbow into his face, lunged out and rammed a shoulder into a yelling cowboy's midriff. He straightened, lifting the man bodily as he rose.

The cowpoke shouted and beat at Santee's shoulders. Baring his teeth with effort, Jim hurled him through the broken window. The cowboy's body took out the remainder of the glass and the flimsy frame. Santee went out after the flailing body, diving through head-first, twisting in mid-air. He lit on his shoulders and it drove breath from him, but he managed to roll away from the light spilling through the window. Guns blasted and the dazed cowboy, sporting a dozen small cuts, staggered up and the shooting ceased as the men inside cursed him for getting in the line of fire.

By the time they ran around and out the front door, Santee was long gone, faded into the blackness beyond the reach of the flames that were now licking up the outside wall of the house, around the shattered office window.

Half-a-dozen guns blazed uselessly into the night.

Dakin, nursing his throbbing arm, was bawling frantically. 'Get some buckets going! Save the ranch! Forget that Injun son of a bitch! Save . . . my . . . goddamn . . . ranch!'

It turned into a mad mêlée, men falling over each other in their eagerness to get water to the seat of the fire.

No one heard Santee's horse carrying him away from Flying D into the night.

10

River Trail

By daylight he was many miles from Flying D.

He watched his backtrail carefully but although he saw a couple of distant riders, no one came close, either to observe, or cause him trouble: maybe too busy still with the fire or its aftermath. If it had got out of control . . .

He hadn't eaten since breakfast the day before and his belly was growling. Shooting small game would have been an easy answer, but he didn't know who the shots might alert. He had no patience with fishing and the few birds he tried hurling sticks at outsmarted him.

The way he wanted to go was down-river: he intended to follow the

Gila's meandering course. It took him close to the Phoenix trail, and his belly growled loud enough, for him to decide to swing more to the west and head for the outskirts of town.

There was a Mexican *cantina* sitting out alone not far from the edge of town and he ate a bowl of chilli while the fat *señora* prepared tortillas that he would take with him to eat cold along the trail. The coffee smelled good and he ordered a cup.

When it came he asked, 'You know anyone named Slocum on the river?'

Her big, round, rheumy eyes suddenly got bigger and rounder. She spilled some coffee, apologized and busied herself mopping up, then made to walk away.

'*Espera, señora, por favor!*' She halted but did not turn.

'I know not this 'Slo-com'. I am very busy, *señor.*'

Quickly, he took some coins from his pocket and jingled them in his hand. She paused, then started forward again.

He dropped the coins one by one on the hardwood counter. She slowly turned to look at the small pile of silver. 'Your *amigo*, this *Slo-com*?'

'Don't know him.'

'I must ask then why you ask about him?'

'I have business with him.' On a hunch he lightly touched his gun butt.

She frowned, sweat sliding across the swarthy, fat face. She seemed to consider just what kind of business Santee might have with Slocum. 'He come from Gila Bend.'

She arched her eyebrows quizzically, looking from the pile of coins to his face. Slowly, he covered the money with his hand, and the disappointment slackened her face.

'Señora, my business will not be to Slocum's advantage.'

The Mexican woman thought about this and the heavy lips moved in a slow smile. '*Bueno*. But, sadly, I can tell you no more. He is — *reservado. Secreto* . . .'

'He travels up and down the river?'

'*Sí*. His kind of business — *extraordinario*, you *comprende*?'

He understood. Running-ironed cattle mixed with a legitimate trail herd and sold at the Phoenix markets. Various goods, including firearms, and sometimes people, smuggled up from or down to the Border on the riverboats. Men of a certain kind with flexible morals could make a good living at such things.

'Gila Bend is Slocum's headquarters? His *cuartel*?'

'*Sí*, his place.' She looked again at the money and he pushed it all across to her. 'He hate all Mexicans.' The coins were quickly scooped into the big apron pocket. Large, crooked teeth flashed at him in a smile. 'I give you some chilli con carne for your travels, and a warning that Slo-com is *muy malo hombre*!'

Santee had already figured that. He was walking to the cantina door when someone called his name.

'Santee! You're taking a chance

comin' back here! Kelly Sanchez'll throw your butt in jail if he sees you.'

It was Carey Brandison, on foot, deputy badge polished and catching the sun in blinding flashes. Santee halted and leaned on the saddlehorn.

'I'll risk Sanchez. You're on the beat early.'

'This is as far as I patrol. Maria there gives me a bowl of chilli to keep me goin', don't you *querida*?' He blew a kiss at the grinning fat woman. 'Stayin' in town long?'

'Don't sound so worried, kid, I'm on my way to Gila Bend. To see a man named Slocum.'

The young lawman's face straightened. 'He's not a man, he's an animal; though that's kind of an insult to animals, come to think of it. Kelly won't let him near Phoenix. Watch your step, Santee, Slocum's a bad bastard and the ones he runs with are worse.'

'Where's he hang out in Gila Bend?'

'A *cantina* called Monasterio.'

'The Monastery?'

Carey smiled. 'Well, ain't no saints there, I can guarantee that. At the river end of Ball Street.'

'This Slocum — he got white hair?'

'No. He's a runt, but a vicious one. Well, good luck, Santee. Oh, Brandy said if I should run into you, to tell you her invitation still stands.'

Santee kept his face sober. 'How she doing?'

'Recovering well. Any message for her?'

Santee frowned. 'Tell her I'll look in on her if I'm able to.' He went to his horse at the hitch rail, stowed his tortillas in the saddle-bags, mounted easily.

Carey tensed. 'Maybe I better come with you.'

'Thanks, kid, but this is my kind of work. Besides, I want to go it alone.'

He wheeled his mount, touching a hand lightly to his hat brim. Carey watched him go, and nodded slowly.

He savvied what Santee meant: he felt responsible for Josh Rankin's death, had failed in his job to protect the boy, so, to set things right, in his eyes at least, he *had* to square things himself even at the risk of his life.

'And there sure is one helluva risk if you're goin' up agin Ben Slocum,' Carey said, half aloud. 'Hey, Maria, how's the chilli comin'? Belly's growlin' like my throat's cut . . . '

★ ★ ★

There was a man sprawled beside the trail, face down, no guns in evidence within reach that he could see. A horse stood a little way off, reins trailing, cropping at a patch of sparse, sun-dried grass. It rolled a vaguely curious eye as Santee reined down at the bend of the trail that had hidden the downed man from his sight until now. His hand dropped to his Colt. The fallen man's hat had been knocked askew and Santee glimpsed the dirty white of a bandage, flaxen hair showing below the edge.

Six-gun in hand, he walked his mount in slowly, sidling up. The hammer spur was under his thumb. He stopped a few yards away, his suspicions confirmed.

The man lying on the ground was Whit Gant. Fresh blood showed on the bandage and there was a thin ribbon of it on the upper side of his face. Santee figured he must have landed head-first when he fell from the saddle. One leg was twisted awkwardly under the big body. He dismounted and approached warily: walked around Gant until he could see his right side where he wore his gun. Gant's limp hand was nowhere near the weapon which was hanging half-out of its holster. He did not react to Santee's probing boot toe and when he was rolled onto his back, his face was grey between the streaks of dust, his eyes closed, one cheek fresh scarred by gravel. Gant had taken quite a tumble. Somehow he had gotten ahead of Santee on the trail to Gila Bend.

Followed him from Flying D but

must have missed the tracks where he'd swung off to Phoenix. Likely looked for a place where he could set-up an ambush, but his fall had put paid to that.

Was that why he was following Santee in the first place? Sent by Dakin to bushwhack him? Could be; that fire must've caused a heap of damage to the ranch house, not to mention Dakin's reputation and standing in the area. Santee had him figured for a vengeful man, despite his high-sounding talk. *But there was something odd about the wealthy rancher, too, something just beneath the surface. Hard to pin down, but there. Almost like some kind of guilt.*

Squatting now, he examined Gant's head wound by lifting an edge of the bandage, noticing how grubby it was close-up. He swore softly. The bullet crease was red and angry-looking at the edges: a sign of infection. He placed a hand on Gant's dirt-caked forehead and felt the heat against his palm.

'You got yourself a high fever, mister. Damn you!'

The bandage was of old rags, torn from a work-shirt by the looks of it, and he figured the cloth must be heavily contaminated with dirt. Likely this had started the infection, spreading rapidly through the big body from the wound, and so close to the brain.

He sat on his hams and rolled a cigarette. Gant lay there, breathing raggedly, moaning once, sweat rolling down his face. Santee drew hard on his smoke and tightened his lips after exhaling.

'You are one buffalo-sized pain in the butt, Gant. I could try to work on you right here but by the look of you, you'd likely up and die before you told me anything useful. Goddammit! Guess I'll have to take you to a sawbones, which means splinting that leg; think I can see a piece of bone poking through . . . *Ah, hell*!'

It was closer to Gila Bend than Phoenix now so it looked like that was where he would have to take the ailing ramrod. Santee looked down at the unconscious man for a long minute, wondering if he was aiding someone who had helped bring about Josh Rankin's death.

There would be hell to pay if that turned out to be the case.

★ ★ ★

Carey Brandison was right, Slocum was a runt. No more than five feet three or four tall, but well-muscled in proportion. He had curly black hair and a beak of a nose that might make a bald eagle jealous. There were sideburns, shaved and upswept to join beneath the nose, making a moustache that spread clear across his narrow face. The chin was dimpled and slightly receding. But it was the gimlet, slushy-brown eyes that drew the attention.

They were what folk called 'bad' eyes and about the baddest Santee had ever seen. They looked at him now without much expression, but it was this very lack that would make a lot of men cringe.

Santee met and held that gaze and the three men seated at the card table with Slocum were surprised to see the tip of his pink tongue flash across his lips, before he cleared his throat and asked in a thin voice, 'I can see you're a 'breed of some kind. But you better not tell me you got any Mex Apache in you.'

'Could have; what difference does it make?'

The bleak eyes burned now and the man on Slocum's right hitched his chair away a foot or more: giving him a cleared space for an easy draw, if necessary.

And it would be necessary if Slocum had his way. Santee could see it coming and didn't aim to dodge it. Slocum shrugged at Jim's casual question. 'I don't like Mexes. If you're *mestizo* they're gonna carry you outa here.'

'Aw, I dunno. Mebbe it's you they'll

carry out — straight to Boot Hill.'

Slocum's eyes pinched down and he set down the greasy cards he had been holding. 'I've about had enough of you, 'breed. Tell me what you want, and I'll decide how you'll leave.' There was a quick, on-off grin, tight and mirthless. '*If* you leave.'

'Josh Rankin.'

Santee watched the face ripple with a shockwave but only briefly. Slocum had control in less than two seconds. One of the men at the table sucked in a quick, sharp breath, but Santee didn't move his gaze from Slocum.

'Who?' the little man asked hoarsely.

'The greenhorn you and your *bravos* set up for a so-called prank with an *hombre* goes by the name of Whitey.'

That name put steel rods in the spines of all four men at the table. The other drinkers in the *cantina* watched silently and tensely: they saw violence about to give birth here and though many were afraid in case bullets flew wild, they were reluctant to leave — no one before this day had ever seen anyone stare down Ben Slocum,

'The hell're you talkin' about?'

'You know, Slocum; Whit Gant told me.'

'That lumberin' son of a bitch! Well, he's good as dead next time I see him.'

'You saying he's lying?'

'That's what I'm sayin'! *'Breed!'*

Here it was! Coming quicker than Santee expected — Slocum had needed hardly any provocation — almost as if he had been expecting it . . . wanted it.

'I reckon you're the liar,' Santee said quietly and Slocum couldn't believe it for a moment. Then he started his draw, small hand blurring to his gun butt. The others at the table leapt to their feet, kicking over their chairs, lifting their guns, doing their best to distract Santee.

Jim's Colt filled his hand smoothly and there was a roar of gunfire and swirling smoke. Through the haze, the gawkers saw men throw up their hands, smashed back by the strike of lead, going down violently. One man doubled up and fell across the table, then rolled to the edge, upsetting the whole shebang, the sound lost in the ear-ringing echoes of the gunfire.

All four men were down. Santee stood there unhurriedly reloading his smoking pistol. There was a fresh red sear across his left cheek where one of Slocum's bullets had come close and a new hole in the brim of his hat. But he was unharmed, stepped over two writhing men — the one who had tipped over the table was sprawled, dead, several crumpled cards spotted with blood resting on his chest.

Ben Slocum had been slammed back against the wall and was sitting on the floor, those slushy brown eyes now milky with pain, a hand pressed into his bleeding chest. A streak of viscous blood crawled from a corner of the razor-slash mouth.

Santee, Colt reloaded and held easily, went down on one knee beside him, staying close to the wall, covering his back. But there didn't seem to be any danger from the on-lookers. He prodded Slocum under the ear with the gun barrel.

'Where's Whitey?'

Slocum shuttled his pallid gaze to Santee's face.

'In — hell 'b-breed. He's . . . always been . . . there . . . '

'Then you'll see him mighty soon — but it could be a rough passage, Slocum.'

'Whole life's been rough . . . I don't care. If I'm . . . goin', I'm . . . goin'. An' I won't tell you a goddam thing!'

An explosive fit of coughing caught him and blood sprayed, forcing Santee to jump back. Slocum's small body racked and twisted and when the coughing had dropped to a wheeze, Santee knew he would get nothing from the man. He swore: he shouldn't have shot so straight. But there had been no time for aiming, not with four different men to watch: shots had to be traded, and quickly, the gun barrel sweeping from target to target through the thickening smoke.

The other man still alive stared with eyes filled with pain, but there was toughness there which changed to a flaring fear when Santee placed his gun muzzle against the bony kneecap, showing through a rent in the stained trousers.

'Tell me about Whitey.'

The man swallowed, eyes bulging as he stared back. Santee didn't hurry him: there was no law in Gila Bend to be worried about and no one in the *cantina* seemed to care that Slocum and his bunch had met their match.

'I dunno nothin'! Ask . . . Dakin.'

'Says he doesn't know him.'

'L-lyin': Whitey's his . . . son.'

'His son?'

The man nodded jerkily, grunting, stifling a cough.

'So they say. Slocum knew. That's all I know — I swear it! I-I need a sawbones . . . ' The man passed out.

Santee's mouth tightened: something

told him it was the truth. He stood but didn't holster the gun as he backed towards the door.

★ ★ ★

The doctor was a harassed-looking man named Waterman. He glared at Santee as he shrugged into his coat and picked up his battered medical bag.

'Business has picked up since you came to town, mister.'

'Three of the men're dead in that *cantina*, Doc. Only one still breathing.'

Waterman grinned as he jammed his hat on his grey head. 'That's OK: I'm the local undertaker, too.'

Santee gave him a faint smile. 'How's Gant? Can I see him?'

'Yes. Fever's not so bad but his leg's giving him a lot of pain. He's had a good dose of willowbark and laudanum so he could be a mite woozy. Try not to kill him before I get back.'

Santee watched the medico hurry out and then found his way towards the rear of the old clapboard house where the infirmary was. There were four iron beds arranged on a rear porch, canvas blinds on rollers all that kept out the weather. But today was sunny and he could smell the river mixed with the odours of sickness as he stepped up to the only occupied bed.

Whit Gant was half-propped up on pillows, his face cleaner but still greyish. The bandage on his head was a lot whiter than the original and his glistening eyes were full of apprehension as Santee approached. His broken leg was in a heavy plaster cast. 'I heard shootin'.'

'Some vermin in the *cantina*. Doc tells me you're in for a rough time, Gant.' Santee didn't know whether that was true or not, but it wouldn't hurt any to unsettle the ramrod a little more.

'Christ! This is rough enough. He says you brung me in — saved my leg, mebbe my life.'

'Only because I want to talk to you.'

Gant's eyes flared a little, but the

man was too fever-weak and feeling bad to have much of the old arrogance and fire. 'Can try — your luck.'

'Aim to.' Santee loosened the Colt in his holster and he saw the sheets move as Gant's body tensed. He sat down in a chair and rolled a cigarette, taking his time, lit up while Gant waited, face tight with anxiety and anger at his own helplessness. 'Dakin send you to bushwhack me?'

Gant's eyebrows rose and his parched-looking lips moved in what might have been a faint smile. He shook his head slowly.

'You got it wrong. Dakin was almighty riled 'cause I told you about the boys gettin' Rankin drunk an' takin' him down to the river — an' I mentioned Slocum, too. Only did it 'cause I figured you'd go hell for leather after Slocum, get you outa our hair, but Heath din' see it that way.' His face darkened. 'He's a mean son of a bitch when he wants! He was ravin' about the fire you started — half the house is gone, all his breedin' an' stock records destroyed — an' all them pictures of Elspeth. Never seen him in such a damn state. Dunno what he's doin', he's so shocked. Hell, he fired me! Me! I been with him nigh on twenty years, doin' his dirty work — '

'And being well paid.'

'Yeah. Money was good. But — Judas! He owes me a lot more'n money, for the things I done for him.'

'Now you owe me. But I'm only interested in what you did to Josh Rankin.'

Gant licked his lips and asked for a drink of water. Santee held the glass while the man gulped it down, spilling some over his stubbled chin. The ramrod looked up at Santee.

'I don't like you much, 'breed.'

'There's a long line ahead of you.'

Gant scowled but it didn't work. He was too weak to handle anger. 'Look, I came after you. Had some idea if I bushwhacked you, it'd put me in good again with Heath. But I missed you somewhere along the trail. I figured to wait, see if you showed, but I come over all dizzy and next thing I know I'm lyin' here with a doctor bendin' over me.'

Santee sat down again, drawing on his cigarette.

'It riled me, Dakin kickin' me out that way.'

'Still riled enough to tell me what I want to know?'

'I'm decidin'.'

'Mebbe this'll help you. One of Slocum's men said Whitey is Dakin's son — start with that.'

11

Whitey

Danny Dakin was six years old and already in love with the Great Outdoors.

Most mornings he was awake at first light, hurriedly pulling on baggy trousers cut down from big brother Luke's, the suspenders worn so that the pants sagged baggily around his knees. Danny didn't care. Barefoot, hatless, snatching a juicy cob from the swaying cornstalks of the field as he rushed by for his breakfast, he would head for the foothills, sometimes carrying his fishing pole or the Indian bow-and-arrows the father of his friend, Squirrel Eye, had made for him.

He enjoyed his lone adventures, enjoyed them more with Squirrel Eye, but most of all when his father took time from rounding-up his cattle herds or other ranch chores and they went hunting.

Heath Dakin was a fine shot and hoped the boy had inherited the trait. Luke, the older son, was only an indifferent shot, would rather read a book or study pages of maths than camp out. The girl, Maureen, naturally showed interest in more feminine things, encouraged by her mother, Elspeth. But she was a fine horse-woman, too, and had entered in that year's Nevada State Fair. They were a happy family.

Heath Dakin liked to think he loved his wife and all his children equally, but there was no doubt his favourite was young Danny-boy, as Heath affection-ately called his youngest son.

'Got promise that lad,' he said, many a time, at hoedowns and community get-togethers. 'A natural outdoorsman. I hope to leave him a fine ranch one of these days.'

'What about Luke and Maureen?'

someone might ask. 'And Elspeth?'

'They'll all be provided for,' Heath replied confidently and a mite edgily. 'I play no favourites.'

But he did, and everyone knew it, even Danny-boy. And, like all six year olds, he traded on it as often as he figured he could get away with it.

Then there came the time they went hunting wild boar in the foothills. Elspeth wanted to hold a social gathering and was determined to make it as different and memorable as she could. Other ranchers' wives always spit-roasted a steer, but she wanted two fat pigs and would serve crackling roast pork with cinnamon-apple sauce and some of her home-made, award-winning apricot chutney.

'We gotta make a good showin', boy,' Heath told Danny as the early morning mist curled around them outside their dew-wet tent. He was cleaning the rifles, a heavy .44/.70 Remington for himself and a lighter Savage for the boy. Aimed well and true, the Savage would stop a charging pig in its tracks every bit as well as the big-bore firearm. And Heath knew Danny wouldn't flinch, would coolly face down any rampant animal in the wild and draw his bead, squeezing off his shot only when he was satisfied he would hit the vital spot.

That was what he did. It was a young boar, tusks short and gleaming white, ready to be blooded. And the pig was eager to rip up human flesh, squealing and snorting as it spotted Danny crouching in the brush. It tore in and Heath rose to shout a warning but Danny was already tracking that pig with the rifle.

The boy stepped out confidently, body-stance correct, as Heath had taught him — left foot forward, knee very slightly bent, right foot flat to the ground, weight on the whole foot, body tilted a shade off the vertical, butt snugged-in, crooked right arm level with the shoulder. With the fore-end of the rifle gripped firmly by the left hand, right index finger curling lightly around the trigger until the foresight blade centred in the V of the rear sight, level with the tops of the V, then . . .

The little Savage cracked and Heath was pleased to see it barely jumped in recoil. Danny-boy had gripped the rifle exactly right. He swept his gaze forward in time to see the charging pig suddenly ram its nose into the dirt, short forelegs folding under it, hairy, mud-spattered body rising up in a series of somersaults until it crashed on its side only a couple of yards from where Danny stood.

He turned his dirt-smeared face towards his father, the freckles seeming to ripple over the dusty skin as he grinned, long, pale hair blowing in the wind.

'I bags a hind-quarter for myself!' he piped cheekily, and ran forward, reaching for his skinning knife.

Then Heath saw the movement in the brush to the left, and knew why the young pig had been so eager to attack: the father boar was watching. Now it came charging out of the bushes, snorting in a rising shrillness of vengeful anger, red-eyed, long curving tusks ready to rip out Danny's innards.

'Danny! Get down, boy!'

Heath shouted urgently and his words reached Danny as the heavy Remington came to Heath's shoulder, muzzle tracking the charging animal at blurring speed.

Danny hadn't seen the boar as it was coming in from his left and slightly behind him. But, as he turned his head to look at his father he glimpsed the pig thundering in. He instinctively propped, dug in his heels, skidding, his small light body, stopping almost immediately.

Heath fired expecting that Danny-boy would keep running, or drop to the ground while he dealt with the boar.

To his horror, Heath Dakin saw the patch of red streak through Danny's pale hair, saw the head jerk violently, the skinny body stumble, then go down as if someone had chopped the boy's legs from under him.

★ ★ ★

Whit Gant was breathing now as if he had run up a mountain and he sagged back against his sweaty pillow, eyes closed. Cigarette burned down, Santee flicked it over the rails past a partly raised canvas blind, and hitched his chair closer to the bed. He got Gant a drink of water and the man took it eagerly. He looked up, eyes red and moist.

'What happened to the boy? Was he OK?'

'You don't get it, do you? Danny-boy is Whitey!' Santee frowned. 'His hair turned pure white while he was recoverin' from that headshot. Heath took him to the best hospitals, mortgaged the ranch to the hilt, had him seen by some of the top medics in San Francisco. Even brought some professor in from England.' He cleared his throat, shook his head. 'Was no good: there was nothin' they could do.'

Frowning, Santee said, 'What're you tellin' me?'

Gant's eyes were a little wide now and his breath came in short gasps. Sweat rolled down his face, soaked his upper body. 'Heath's bullet damaged Danny's brain. Can't remember what it was called.'

'Irreversible brain damage?'

'Somethin' like that. They wanted to put him in some place for crazy people, an asylum. Judas, they say Heath almost killed that damn professor for suggestin' it. Took three guards to pull him off. Elspeth near went crazy, too. They put in some really hard times doin' what they could for him, but they knew nothin' an', eventually, they had to admit Danny-boy was gonna be queer for the rest of his life. It was sure rough on them, carin' for him. Heath almost killed himself with work, made a lot of money, some say by rustlin' but no one's ever proved it — and you'll get nothin' outa me about it.' He looked squarely at Santee when he said that.

It was as good as an admission Gant had helped with some rustling, but that made no nevermind here . . .

Heath and Elspeth did their best to care for the boy themselves, but there was no one they could turn to for help. Virtually all they could do was see he was fed and kept clean — and try to cope with explosive tantrums that left all three exhausted. Danny was rapidly growing up, causing a whole new set of problems: a child's body with adult demands and a mind that could never control those demands — a *vicious* child's mind, as it turned out.

They brought in nurses to look after him, but he was more than the nurses could handle. Danny would go completely off his head at times when his frustration became intolerable. Near killed one of the nurses, carved up the face of a whore Heath hired for him, thinking — correctly — that maybe the boy-man had adult-type itches that needed scratching.

Santee felt uneasy about all this. To his surprise — and alarm — he found himself feeling a strange compassion for the once-cheerful young boy, who, through no fault of his own, had developed into a monster.

Gant's voice was hoarse now and he shivered from time to time, jumped when sudden pain speared through his shattered leg.

'Danny grew to manhood and the 'man' part turned out to be a big piece of his trouble — you know what I mean?'

Santee could guess, after what had happened to Josh.

'Well, it was just one more problem they had to deal with. Elspeth never let Heath forget he'd fired the shot. He was goin' through hell and she made his life even worse, but he worshipped that woman almost as much as the boy. She got real sick and on her death-bed she made him swear that he would look after Danny for the rest of his life: if Heath died first, Luke and Maureen would have to take care of him, even though Danny was a big-grown man by now and they might have lives of their own to lead. Heath made his promise, and he kept it.'

'And Danny became Whitey?'

Gant nodded, touched his head. 'No one is allowed to call him Danny, only Heath. Some crazy notion he got into his head. I mean, the strain told on him, too, and he changed from the Heath I first knew. For years he's kept Whitey locked up in a special cabin back of the spread. Lets him out now and again — *has* to let him out or Whitey's like to kick the cabin to matchwood. He's mighty strong and mean when he's in one of his moods, but most times he's not too bad, just like a kid. He likes bein' with the boys, those of us that Heath trusts to keep the secret. Has to quieten him down with laudanum, though, sometimes. Hefty doses, too.'

'What d'you mean 'lets him out'?'

'Well, them urges he gets are pretty rough. So we — Heath gets us to set up somethin' for him: a bunch of us take him down by the river for a party. We pour a load of booze into some ranny we've picked up from one of the saloons and, afterwards — fifty bucks usually fixes things so there's no fuss.'

'I ought to kill you where you lie, you son of a bitch! This is what you did to Josh, ain't it? Got him drunk and . . . Except he wouldn't need, or take, any money!'

Gant went very still and silent as he saw Santee's face: there was pure lust for murder there. Gant shivered and nodded, the fear all through him now. 'We — Well, he was good company, Josh, willin' to join in the fun.'

'Fun! For Chris'sakes! You think that kinda thing was *fun*?' Santee was striding back and forth now, barely holding in his rage. 'Hell, Gant, I dunno why I don't shoot you!'

'I-I can tell you where Whitey is now.'

Santee stopped pacing, glared. 'He's not locked in his cabin at Flying D?'

'Hell, no, not after what happened — to that gal as well as Josh. I mean, Slocum urged him on at the sandbar, bein' the kinda son of a bitch he was, but — Heath panicked when he found out Josh was to've been the governor's brother-in-law, wanted to get Whitey out of the way. Feller named Walt Bascombe used to work for Heath — '

'I know him — Sheriff of Yuma now.'

'Yeah, well, he has a half-brother runs the prison there. Heath made a deal for 'em to keep Whitey in the solitary section until things quieten down. Cost Heath plenty to fix it, too. Whitey'll be on his way down the river soon as they figure it's safe to move him.'

No wonder Bascombe nearly jumped out of his skin when Santee suggested he might have been on that river-bank with Whitey and the others.

'Who else was on the river-bank? You and your men?'

'Judas, no, that was Slocum's crew. Heath hired him to smuggle Whitey downriver in one of his boats. They were holdin' him on that sandbar till the boat was ready — had more cargo to load. Wouldn't've been any trouble if

Josh hadn't tracked Whitey down and tried to kill him.'

Well, Slocum and his men had paid the price . . . but what was he going to do about Whitey?

The man should be locked away where he could never do anyone any harm. He could even get worse. Santee once again felt the touch of that unwanted sympathy for the man, but *he was a killer! The one who had murdered Josh Rankin in cold blood, and that innocent girl who had happened to see it all. Maybe Slocum had done the urging, but Whitey had done the deed.*

Santee recalled Senator Rankin's words to him as he started out on the assignment.

'*Track down that killer and don't worry about bringing him to trial: kill the bastard where he stands! Don't bury him: leave him to the wolves and vultures — I want him* obliterated.'

Santee had felt the same way when he had set out.

Now? Well, no doubt the best solution all round was for Whitey to die. But Santee couldn't quite shake the picture of the happy, carefree six-year-old Gant had described — Danny Dakin, a cheeky, freckle-faced, barefoot boy, bursting with the joy of life — in an instant hurtled into the bleak, tortured world that was the twisted mind of Whitey Dakin.

At six, Santee had been happy, too, learning the Indian ways. He had a special friend, a year or so older, Fat Beaver. The chubby, clumsy little Sioux boy was everyone's favourite. He tried hard to keep up with the young warriors-in-training. Then, one time he fell into a river, failed to surface as the current carried his plump body away. Tall Beaver, the boy's father, finally rescued him, but the boy was unconscious. He was strung up by the heels, pummelled to expel the water from his lungs, while the medicine man sang for his salvation. He revived, but was never again the same clumsy, likeable and laughing playmate Santee had known.

The Sioux believed his mind had been claimed by the Spirits. Years later, a cavalry doctor told Santee that Fat Beaver had been submerged too long without breathing: probably, the lack of oxygen had killed some of his brain cells. It turned him into a sullen, jealous, tantrum-throwing stranger, shunned, regarded with suspicion — until, one day he threw a girl child into the river. Unable to swim she had drowned, her struggles vastly amusing to Fat Beaver, dancing with excitement on the bank.

Tribal law demanded he die. Like the old and sick who could not keep up with the tribe on its wanderings, Fat Beaver was abandoned to his fate in inhospitable country without food or water.

'This is our law,' Tall Beaver explained solemnly.

'But he can't help it!' Santee had exclaimed, not understanding. He had tried to take him food, but had been forcibly restrained and severely reprimanded. Moving on with the tribe, *afraid and sobbing for his friend, he kept looking back — until the black dots of vultures spiralled across the hot skies. Far into adulthood, he could still hear those pitiful, wailing cries coming out of the night, reminding him that he had done nothing to help his helpless friend: nothing!*

★ ★ ★

As soon as Gant had begun telling his story about Danny-boy, Santee's mind had filled with Fat Beaver's fate. Even now, thirty years later, it sometimes came in the night to jar him awake in sweating terror with Fat Beaver's name on his lips.

'Heath knows Whitey's a danger to everyone as long as he's alive,' Gant's voice slowly intruded into his mind, almost as if he had read Santee's thoughts. 'But he won't let no harm come to him because of that deathbed oath he made Elspeth. I think there's times when Heath'd like to kill the boy himself and be done with it all, but he won't take that way out, neither.'

Gant was mighty exhausted by now, looked out of his fever-bright eyes at Santee. 'I've said enough, 'breed. You saved my neck; now I've squared with you. Get the hell outa here an' lemme get some sleep.'

★ ★ ★

Leaving, Santee met the medico at the front gate. The doctor lifted a hand, halting him.

'I think I'd better keep you around, young feller.'

'How's that, Doc?'

'Keep you on to kill off all the bad *hombres* in this town. You'd have plenty of work.'

'Three dead and one wounded's enough for me, Doc.' Santee started walking but paused as the sawbones called after him,

'I treated the one you left alive, mean type, ungrateful: he gave me the slip when he said he needed the privy . . . Slocum and the other two had most of this town scared white for years. Everyone's glad they're dead, but they don't want 'em planted just yet.'

Santee frowned, curious now.

'They're on show, in their coffins, at the carpenter's store for a few days. Ten cents admission.'

Santee nodded. 'I seen the Cole Brothers like that in Wichita, after Marshal Forrest Wedemeyer ambushed 'em robbin' the bank, but he charged a quarter to look.'

'Did he, by God! Well, I'll soon set that right!'

Waterman dashed off and Santee continued on. When he reached the main drag he was surprised to see the winding queues of folk lining up to view the men he had killed. He crossed the street, and was halfway, when a gun blasted. Instinctively, he ducked and shoulder-rolled into a gutter as the bullet shattered the display window of a haberdashery storefront. A second bullet kicked stones against his chest as he spun on his belly, palming up his six-gun, searching for the shooter.

The folk waiting to see Slocum and his companions had scattered, running for cover. He couldn't see anyone with a gun. Then another bullet flung dirt against his neck. He rolled swiftly, loosing off two shots, high, but in the general direction of where the crowds had been.

Someone was crouched behind a large waterbutt near the general store. He glimpsed the shoulder of a cream shirt, the brim of a dark-brown hat. Then the muzzle of a rifle swung in his direction. He fired. The bullet hit one of the metal binding bands, snarled away, striking sparks.

As he began sprinting across there was a faint yell and a body tumbled into view, struggling to scramble under cover again. Santee involuntarily broke his stride: it was a woman shooting at him!

A small gloved hand reached for the

fallen rifle. He kicked the weapon out of reach. The woman snatched a small pistol from her belt, thrusting it almost in his face. He wrenched his head aside as she fired. It was a small calibre — likely .36, possibly only a .32 — but he felt the scorch of the muzzle flash. Head ringing, he wrested the pistol from her. She immediately flew at him, clawed fingers reaching for his eyes. He wrenched his head back. She struggled and tried to bite his wrist, the hat falling off, revealing a swirl of raven-black hair. He thrust her from him and she tried to snatch a knife from a belt sheath. *That was enough!*

He slapped her, open-handed, maybe harder than he meant to. Her feet left the ground and he kept her from falling. She sagged against him. A small crowd had gathered and Santee looked around at the gawking faces. 'Anyone know this crazy woman?'

There was a brief silence, some murmurings but nothing clear. Then a man wearing a floursack apron over his clothes said, hesitantly, looking strangely at the girl, 'She came into my store earlier an' bought some things, trail stuff, mostly, a few cartridges — and some dynamite. I'm pretty sure she was here a few weeks ago. In fact, I reckon she's the one who was attacked on the sandbar and throwed in the river. Everyone said she was dead, but this sure looks like her.'

12

Wildcat II

Her name was Catriona Montego. When she finally told him, she almost spat the words at him, green eyes cold and murderous, small hands feeling around her belt for any weapons he may have missed.

But Santee had been careful to search her thoroughly — *thoroughly* — to make sure she was not concealing anything lethal anywhere on her person.

Out in the street, he had thrown her over one shoulder, gathered up her weapons, and carried her into the rear of the livery stables where he dumped her unceremoniously on a pile of hay. The hostler came running, saw Santee and nodded slowly. 'Oh, it's you. That's OK, anythin' for the man who killed Slocum.'

As the man hurried off Santee saw that the girl was coming round and he asked her name quickly: this was the best moment for interrogation, when the off-guard victim would give an automatic reponse, nearly always honestly.

As soon as she spoke she realized he had tricked her and her eyes chilled, faculties rapidly returning now. He glimpsed the small pendant on a silver chain around her neck — a caricatured laughing cat. He reached for it and she pressed back into the hay, slapping his hand aside. 'Don't touch me!'

'Just wanted to see your pendant.'

A slight frown appeared between those disconcerting eyes. 'It is of no interest to anyone but me.'

'I heard of one like that; it was in the saddle-bags on a dead horse with the brand of two Xs inside a triangle. I've a feeling your mount carries the same brand.'

'Of course. It is our *rancho*'s brand, in Sonora. But I tell you nothing more

— I just want to kill you!'

'Why? I had nothing to do with what happened to you on that sandbar.'

She stared back, and a slow smile touched her lips. 'Ah! You think I am *fantasma*, eh?'

'No, I don't think you're a ghost, but I sure as hell wonder how you survived what those scum did to you and then — the river! How come you didn't drown?'

'Perhaps because I was never in the river.'

'A witness saw them throw you in — unconscious.'

She was sober now, the eyes narrowed. 'You speak of Lita — my sister.'

It was a like a blow to the solar plexus. For a moment he couldn't get a breath: he simply stared. Her eyes! *Green!* Navajo Joe had said, 'Her eyes were like cold, grey ice'. 'You and your sister are — were — twins?'

She nodded, full lips forming a tight little rose now beneath the slightly turned-up nose. 'Identical. And like so many twins, we had a mysterious — *armonia — afinidad*. I do not know your word . . .'

'Harmony, affinity — I've heard of it. One twin has a bellyache and the other, even a hundred miles away, will have the same symptoms, or at least sense there is something wrong with the other one.'

She nodded slowly, regarding him somewhat more warily now. 'You *comprende!*' She looked very sad now. 'I knew something bad — evil — had happened to Lita when she does not come back. It distress me. My father call doctors; they cannot tell what is wrong with me. I cannot eat; I am restless, not sleeping *I know Lita has come to a great deal of harm!*' She drew a deep breath. 'I decide I must find her. But first I have our *segundo* teach me how to shoot properly.'

'You came up the Arizona Trail, alone? Started searching for Lita?'

That's what she had done: this young woman, beautiful but deadly, had traipsed the treacherous and bloody trails up through strange renegade-infested country, searching for some sign of her sister, Lita, with whom she had some kind of spiritual connection: a mysterious trait with some twins, especially identical ones, that had confounded science for centuries and would continue to do so far into the future.

There was no logical explanation, but it was *real*: it had been effectively demonstrated thousands of times.

'What was Lita doing up here in the first place?'

'She have a friend who say she find her good work in a big *rancho* as a *institutriz* . . . ?'

'Governess.'

Her face hardened. 'Lita was tired of our *rancho*, have big fight with our padre, and she leave. But the 'friend' lie! It is *burdel* — bordello — where she want Lita to work. She ask me, too, but I not trust her.'

'Lita must've decided to follow the

river back to the Border after leaving this so-called 'friend' and ran afoul of Whitey Dakin.'

Catriona tensed. '*Sí*! That name I hear, too. I try to find him. Then I learn this man Slocum, who know about this Whitey, have been killed by a half-breed.' She went on, tight-lipped. 'I am very angry! The man I need to tell me where to find the one who murder my Lita and someone already kill him before I speak with him!'

'So, you started pot-shotting at me — you're a damn wildcat. Seems to run in the family.'

Her eyes were green slits now. She fingered the pendant roughly. 'Our padre call us, Lita and me, his 'little wildcats'. He give us each one of these.' She paused. 'You — Santee — I have calm down now. I have been foolish.' He smiled thinly: he bet that cost her something to say! 'You will take me to this Whitey now? We will kill him together, if you say, but I rather do it myself. OK?'

'Not OK, Catriona. I don't know where Whitey is — now hold it! You try to rip my eyes out and I'll damn well shoot you! I mean it!'

She backed off, bosom heaving against her cream shirt. 'Why you lie to me?'

'I'm not lying. Look. I'll tell you as much as I know — will you listen without going loco?'

Tight-lipped, she said, 'If you lie — if I *think* you lie, I will kill you!'

'*Judas!*' he breathed. 'OK, here it is ...'

It took longer than he figured, even heavily editing the story about Josh and his own tracking down of the killer.

'All I know now is he's on his way to Yuma Prison. The warden is gonna lock him away in the punishment cells until they figure it's safe to take him back to Flying D.'

'This loco one must die!'

'He'd be better off dead, I guess, but — he's kind of a tragic case, too, Catriona.'

'Ah! You *Americanos*! Too damn soft! So, he was nice little *muchacho* and his *padre* shoot him in the head and now he *muy malo*! You look wrong, Santee! It not what he was, it what he *is! Now*! He kill my dear sister, my Lita — ' Her voice broke and she paused to brush at one eye, nostrils flaring slightly. 'He is her killer — she die terribly. *He* will die terribly, too!'

Santee had never had any doubts before about hunting down killers or outlaws, or trading lead with them, shooting to kill. Right or wrong were clear in his mind, no doubts. But this just seemed — if not wrong, not quite right somehow. He had thought the world of young Josh Rankin and he would not let the boy's death go unavenged, but something was working in him, something that made him hesitate where Whitey was concerned. Not all the blame should lay with Whitey — no more than it had with Fat Beaver. Whitey Dakin had been locked away until the pressures became so great that he could no longer cope, or be ignored. But Dakin had given him all the wrong kind of attention during those crises.

It was twenty years since young Danny Dakin had been headshot; medicine had made many advances during that time.

Whitey, murderous and depraved as he was, should have some chance: he didn't know why. It was all mixed up in his head with Fat Beaver and the boy having no say in his eventual fate, and he not being able — or too cowardly — to help him. Even if it was little more than a token attempt to make up for what had been denied Fat Beaver, it seemed to Santee, Whitey at least should be given that chance.

'We'll track down this Whitey, all right, Catriona.'

'We must do it quickly, then. Once he is in Yuma Prison, we will not be able to reach him.'

There were ways, even in a place like Yuma, but he said nothing about them.

'I need to get in touch with the governor, Catriona. He's a humane man and can arrange for Whitey to be seen by one of the top men who know his type of affliction. Or he can arrange for him to be committed to some place that will at least try to help him.'

She drew herself up to her full height, brushing straw from her clothes. She stopped the action, looking at him steadily. 'You are blind, Santee! Whitey killed your friend! He raped and tortured my sister! If he was a pet dog that suddenly started attacking everyone, he would be shot!'

'That doesn't work, Catriona. Whitey doesn't understand what he's doing. He savvies it gives him gratification, but he doesn't realize he's doing wrong. He doesn't even savvy what is wrong or right. And that's Dakin's fault, not Whitey's.'

'Uh! You are a fool! Soft! He kills so he must be killed! *And I will see to it!* If you try to stop me, you, too, will die!'

She meant it, he had no doubt about that.

She began to gather up her rifle and the small pistol, slipping the knife into her belt sheath. He watched her carefully, hand on gun butt.

'I unloaded your guns.'

The green eyes were murderously cold. 'When I need them, my guns will be loaded,' she said with a good deal of contempt. 'If you see me again, you should remember that, Santee.'

He watched her turn abruptly and walk away, down the wide aisle, out through the big double doors to the street.

It was nearing sundown, shadows beginning to thicken. The hostler appeared, holding a two-pronged hay fork, smiling crookedly.

'No luck, huh? Them Mex gals are hard to figure. One minute they're all hot 'n' cosy, next — '

The breath gusted out of him as Santee poked stiffened fingers into the man's midriff, and walked out.

238

★ ★ ★

He went back to The Monastery *cantina* at the end of Ball Street. There was still someone who might be able to tell him where Whitey was and he might get to him before the girl. *So beautiful yet so damned deadly!*

Deep down, he felt Whitey would have to die, but the poor bastard *did* deserve some sort of chance! Almost forty years old with the mentality of a spoilt brat! There had to be some reckoning — somehow. *And, also, a debt to be paid.*

The place was smoky, lantern-lit against the encroaching darkness, noisy with drinkers and card players. No one recognized him when he first entered: it was too smoky and, truth be known, few cared who patronized the *cantina* except maybe the owner. He was behind the counter, cutting down on expenses by working bar himself. His name was Calhoun, big-shouldered, dark-red hair plastered across his scalp.

239

He pumped a beer into a frothing glass, filled it with amber all the way to the top, and had it resting on a bar towel when Santee reached the counter,

'On the house. We ain't missin' Slocum's custom.' Santee nodded his thanks and drank thirstily. 'Been to see the bodies yet?'

Santee shook his head. 'I've seen enough bodies. But I hear the one I wounded skipped on Doc Waterman.'

'Yeah, Lance Mooney. Would sell out his grandmother if it suited him, but he's a hard bastard, too, almost as tough as Slocum was. They was good pards, so I'd watch my back if I was you.'

'You think he's still around?'

The man hesitated, uneasy with the question. 'Well, that I wouldn't know; I was just talkin' general-like.'

'Doc says Mooney's hit in the side and neck. He's likely to bleed plenty if he keeps runnin', so maybe he'll go to ground somewhere close.'

'Yeah — mebbe. But Mooney don't

have many friends in this town. Specially now Slocum's not here to back him up. I reckon he'd make a run for it right away.'

Santee drained the glass, shook his head when the man made signs for a refill. 'That hit the spot. Need a room for the night, though. What you got spare upstairs?'

The man was suddenly cagey. 'Well, not much — I mean, *nothin'*. Word spread about Slocum an' t'others bein' on display and folk from the ranches roundabout have hit town to come have a peek-see.' He grinned tightly. 'You makin' this town a lot of money one way an' t'other. Sorry, can't help you with a room.'

'How about that lean-to you got out back?'

'Well, there's a feller does some work for me.' He winked ponderously. 'An' sometimes he needs to stay outa sight for a while. Lean-to's for him.'

'Occupied at the moment?'

The barkeep lowered his voice,

nodding. 'Don't spread it around though — some hard *hombres*'re lookin' for him right now.'

'Seems plenty big — maybe I could spread my bedroll in there.'

'Christ, no! He'll kill anyone tries to walk in without my say-so. Sleeps with a loaded sawn-off.'

'Mighty dangerous. OK. I'll find somewhere to lay down the weary bones. Thanks for the beer.'

He went out the front door and immediately he was out of sight, the barkeep called over one of the saloon loungers. 'Bushy, go to the lean-to and tell Mooney Santee's lookin' for him. Hurry!'

Bushy was facing the front, looking past Calhoun's shoulder, and the sudden alarm on the man's face made the *cantina* man stop speaking, turn swiftly.

Santee was halfway back to the bar, left forefinger wagging in a 'naughty-naughty' sign. Calhoun panicked and reached under the bar for his shotgun,

Bushy diving for the floor, wanting no part in this.

Santee's Colt came up blazing and Calhoun reeled back into the shelves, bottles falling and smashing. The shotgun discharged wildly into the end of the bar, scattering men and their drinks as splinters thrummed. Calhoun tried to bring the shotgun around to fire the second barrel at Santee, who triggered, seeing his bullet drive the man down with a clatter. And then he was running for the back door, yelling, 'Get outa my way!'

Men trying to clear the bar scattered and he smashed open the flimsy door, turned towards the lean-to. A crouching man came out, gun braced into his side, triggering four fast, hammering shots as he made a faltering lunge for the corner.

Santee staggered, went down, sprawling, firing twice, but he passed out before he saw his bullets cut down Mooney in his tracks.

★ ★ ★

When he awoke, the first person he saw was Whit Gant lying in his bed with his plastered leg and a thick bandage around his head. The man was smoking, looked better than the last time.

He raised his voice: 'Doc! He's come round!' Then, more quietly, he said, 'They didn't think you were gonna make it for a while . . . Mooney got you in the chest.'

'That much . . . I know,' Santee wheezed, feeling the tightness in his upper chest, a metallic taste in his mouth.

Doc Waterman bustled in. 'Well, when I said we ought to keep you around, I didn't mean like this.'

Santee looked up at him and remained silent while the doctor examined him. There was a rubber tube growing out of one side of his chest. 'The hell's that?'

'Drainage, my friend. But you're on the mend now — I'll take the tube out tomorrow. It's been in long enough to come away freely, now.'

'How — how long've I been here?'

'Four days coming up — why? You have some place you'd rather be?'

'Damn right. Did I kill Mooney?'

'Yes, but not right away. He took another day to go. Very tough man. He's on display with his friends now.'

'Hell, I wanted to ask him which one of Slocum's boats was heading down-river for Yuma.'

'He probably could've told you. In fact, I believe he did tell that Mexican girl before she left.' As Santee's jaw dropped, the medic added, 'The one who tried to shoot you? She insisted on nursing Mooney while I was busy trying to save you. Very helpful.'

'God-dammit to hell!'

'Here, here! Don't get excited now, it won't do you any good. Anyway there's no point.'

Santee frowned. 'No point? To what?'

'Getting worked up about the boat. I don't know what your interest in it was, but it blew up a few miles this side of Yuma.'

Santee froze. 'Blew up?'

'Yes. Must've been carrying firearms or explosives. Being one of Slocum's you could never tell what cargo might've been on board.'

'Even a few sticks of dynamite,' Santee said bitterly. 'Any survivors?'

'Not a single one. All blown to bits.'

Santee slumped. 'She sure must've moved fast . . .'

'What? Oh, that Mex girl — she left this for you. Just some gewgaw, but rather novel. You may know what it means.'

Doc took Santee's right hand and placed a slim chain with a glinting pendant on it. 'A laughing cat — though I don't believe I've ever seen a live one that laughs.'

'A wildcat, more like it,' Santee said, half-aloud, closing his fist weakly around the charm. 'A damn *wildcat*!'

THE END

We do hope that you have enjoyed reading this large print book.

Did you know that all of our titles are available for purchase?

We publish a wide range of high quality large print books including:
Romances, Mysteries, Classics
General Fiction
Non Fiction and Westerns

Special interest titles available in large print are:
The Little Oxford Dictionary
Music Book, Song Book
Hymn Book, Service Book

Also available from us courtesy of Oxford University Press:
Young Readers' Dictionary
(large print edition)
Young Readers' Thesaurus
(large print edition)

For further information or a free brochure, please contact us at:
Ulverscroft Large Print Books Ltd.,
The Green, Bradgate Road, Anstey,
Leicester, LE7 7FU, England.
Tel: (00 44) **0116 236 4325**
Fax: (00 44) **0116 234 0205**

LAST MILE TO NOGALES

Ryan Bodie

Nogales was a hell town, in the heart of the desert. Its single claim to fame was its band of deadly guns-for-hire who lived there, especially Ryan Coder, whom some saw as the gun king. Yet Coder found his life on the line when he hired out to the king of Chad Valley and was pitted against Holly, the youngest and deadliest gunslinger of them all. Would Coder end up just another notch on Holly's gun?

THE DEVIL'S RIDER

Lance Howard

When vicious outlaw Jeremy Trask escapes the hangman's noose, he rides into Baton Ridge on a mission of revenge and bloodlust. It had been a year since he'd murdered manhunter Jim Darrow's brother in cold blood. Now, along with the sole survivor of the massacre, a young homeless widow named Spring Treller, Darrow vows to hunt down the outlaw — this time to finish him for good. But will he survive the deadly reception the outlaw has waiting?

SHOWDOWN AT PAINTED ROCK

Walt Masterson

When a wagon train is trapped by armed men in Painted Desert, mountain man Obadiah Peabody helps out. He believes they are all just another bunch of pilgrims aiming for California. But among the innocent travellers are the Driscoll brothers — the meanest bunch of owlhoots. Obadiah realises he's got a tiger by the tail when the brothers turn on their rescuer and kidnap his adopted granddaughter. Can Obadiah succeed against seemingly impossible odds? Can he even survive?